Weaving the Unraveling

HEIDI A. ECKERT

Sand
ISLAND

Published by
Sand Island Publishing
Nashville, TN 37205
United States of America

Cover and Book Design by GKS Creative

ISBN 978-0-9887591-0-7

Library of Congress information on file with Publisher
Weaving the Unraveling/by Heidi A. Eckert

Printed in the USA
First Printing

ISLAND

Weaving the Unraveling

THE DREAM

How could she know at age eighteen that he is the one love she will never forget? A true and enduring love filled with promise, youthful excitement, and playful exploration wrapped in the thrill and risk of being discovered. He, the one who haunts her dreams and pulls her back to recall the honesty of innocence, unbridled passion, and affection, surviving undimmed by years of rejection, lies, and the absence of intimacy. The longing remains unfulfilled, as the dream returns on this lonely night. Can it be the past once again taunting her, or did she choose this, hoping not to face what has yet to be resolved.

In her bed, the blankets weigh heavy on Anna's body as she struggles for peaceful rest. And still the dream occurs, uninvited, never changing. She is chasing him and calling out to him to wait for her. Why can't he see or hear her as she desperately tries to reach him? Yet she continues the pursuit, begging for forgiveness, longing to hold him and melt the years away. To consummate all that was left waiting to be enjoyed. Finally, she reaches him and into his arms she falls. She feels so safe and at home in his arms, at long last he is hers. As calmness envelops her soul, she savors the security and warmth of his body, the scent of his skin.

From the misty background of the dream, his wife appears. Taking his hand, she pulls him away. He briefly looks back at Anna before disappearing into the blackness of the night. Once again, she wakes tearfully, longing for what was once and never forgotten.

Chapter One

Mobile, Alabama, 1977

THE WHEELS OF HIS LIME-GREEN Plymouth Duster, with one working door, headed south toward the bay. The passenger side door would not open so he always held the driver's door for her as she slid in halfway to be as close to him as possible. As the wind blew through the open windows, he reached over and placed his arm around her, pulling her closer to him, steering the car with his left hand. The amber of the caution light ahead turned to red as he slowed to stop at the otherwise dark intersection on Range Line Road. His hand moved from her shoulder to the back of her neck as he pulled her mouth to his. At every red light, they kissed. It was his way. As his lips lingered on hers, cars behind them honked to let them know the light had turned green, but they were in no hurry.

She brushed his brown hair from his face as he kissed her and recalled how just six months earlier they had met. She crossed the campus green, lamenting the fact that her freshman college plans had been interrupted by a family move to the Deep South. Giving up her decision to enter a university in the Midwest, she reluctantly followed her family. Everything about this new town was different from the Midwestern city she had left behind. The air was heavy with humidity and the smell of sulfur from the paper mills that dotted the coast. The scent invaded everything, emphasizing the strangeness of this new place.

Spanish moss hung from the trees and swayed in the breeze as Anna heard someone running behind her. "Please wait," called a voice in a deep Southern drawl, "I have been trying to catch up to you."

Feeling a hand pull her arm, Anna spun around as the breeze caught his brown hair, tossing it wildly across his face, but through it she saw the most brilliant blue eyes that rivaled the November sky above them. A bead of sweat fell slowly from his temple as she found herself consumed by his eyes.

Tanned and tall, he was confident and alarming in a way that whispered to her, an air of danger or intoxication. She found herself immediately drawn to him. His hair curled around the collar of his unbuttoned brown and black buffalo plaid shirt. A white T-shirt hugged his muscular build underneath. His blue jeans were too tight and too short, suggesting that last year's clothes were grabbed in a rush to make it to early classes.

"We have math class together, and I have been trying to talk to you for weeks, but you walk so fast," he laughed. "Why the hurry?"

He had noticed her. She had not noticed him, but at that moment, as he released her arm and his eyes held her gaze, she knew she would never be the same.

The date was made for Saturday night, November sixth, and what followed was a love of two years that would hold on in her memory to fill the next thirty years of emptiness.

She was tall, willow-thin with long golden blonde hair that glistened with highlights from her summer visits to the beach. Her brown, doe-like eyes sparkled with delight when pleased. And he pleased her.

He was the son of a working-class Catholic family with seven children. The family's roots were firmly planted in this community. He grew up ensconced in the heart of this town: the bayous, rivers, beaches, Mardi Gras, Catholic high school, and confession. He worked at the local grocer throughout high school and now college; earning every cent he had while giving a portion to his parents to help support their large family. He didn't care what anyone thought of him; he walked with determination through his life. He worked hard for what he wanted: his engineering degree, and her.

Her family was upper middle class, and while she worked in a dress shop it was mostly for extras, such as clothes and her car payment. College represented a new host of challenges. The ease with which she coasted through high school was gone, and the new classes bored her. Her plans for a career and for her future were unclear to her. However, her parents had always insisted on college for their children. Having lived through the Depression Era as young children, they saw college as the means to a secure future and a way to prevent the hardships they had once known. Anna dutifully attended her classes even though she was unclear as to what path to follow. That is, until she met him.

The honking became more persistent as he released his kiss and laughed out loud. He waved the impatient drivers to pass and drove on into the darkness, turning left on Highway 193. A blinking light in the distance lay at the road's end. Two churches sat on opposite corners of the intersection ahead. A derelict produce stand encased by a wire fence occupied a third corner. He turned and slowed the car almost to a crawl, searching the field beyond the parking lot of Our Lady of the Sea Catholic Church.

He pulled the car off the two-lane road onto what appeared to Anna to be a grass-covered driveway. Almost immediately, he stopped the car to unlock a gate that straddled the driveway several yards from the main road. As he opened the car door, an overture of insects reached a frenzied crescendo as some darted into the car to follow the light. He returned quickly, shifting the car into first gear, then second. The tires of his car crushed oyster shells that lined the bumpy driveway down which they slowly progressed. The sounds of insects rattled through the overgrown trees and bushes that scraped and scratched the car as it passed. The car slipped deeper down the long drive, kicking up white dust from the shells that crushed beneath.

The ever-present haze of humid air blurred the light beaming from the headlights. It was not a misty rain, not fog: the air became weighted with moisture as they got closer to the bay, hanging heavy. The sour smells of paper mills were soon replaced by the fresh scent of salt, fish, and Mobile Bay, which lay ahead, and the heady aroma from the flowering ligustrum bushes that buffered the property.

Pale evening light exposed a small white cottage ahead. The roof was green, and loose shingles hung from the rafters and gutters. A screen door clung by one hinge above the cinder block stairs. He pulled past the structure into the front yard, the bay now visible, the water black and calm. A sliver of moon drew a path across the bay but was swallowed up by the heavy haze, blurred and jagged. He leaped from the car again and said he would return. She was left waiting in the front seat, car headlights ablaze, watching as he disappeared into the night, down the long gray weathered dock, as if to slip into the bay.

There was no light save the beams from the car, and the moon. She no longer saw his outline on the horizon and she considered getting out of the car. The night sounds grew louder as the insects' chorus rang into the night. The humidity and the warmth of the closed car became oppressive. Anna wanted to unroll the car windows but as the sounds magnified around her, fear started to take hold, and she hesitated.

"Where are we?" she said out loud to herself. "And where did he go?" Minutes passed and still she could not make out his shape returning up the dock.

"The crab traps were empty," he announced, breaking the silence and pulling open the car door. "It's still too early in the season."

Her heart was pounding wildly as she tried to understand just what he was telling her. "What?"

"The crab traps," he said. "I walked to the end of the dock to check."

"We drove all this way to catch crabs?" she questioned.

"No," he laughed in the special way that signaled to her his loving amusement. "If you are going to live in Mobile, you will have to learn about crabbing and shrimping!"

He pulled his car around to the back of the cottage and took her hand to lead her out of the car. "I want you to see this place. It belongs to my grandparents, but someday I will own it. This will be my home, here on the bay."

The light provided by the car beams was gone as he fumbled for the keys to the old cottage, opening the door. She immediately noticed the damp musty smell of old life vests, beach towels, and patio cushions, and the staleness of a home not opened for months. A cockroach ran across the floor, making her shudder. Though she had come to know these huge bugs were a part of Deep South living, she was repulsed every time she encountered one.

The back door opened into a small kitchen with an old stove and a farmhouse wash sink. The floor creaked and sank under their weight as he led her through the house describing, each room as he went. The center room was a family room, sparsely furnished with two small patio sofas pushed against the walls. The cushions were covered in a plastic fabric of time-faded flowers reminiscent of the styles popular in the 1950s. A cream-colored slipcover that was too small tried to camouflage the cushions' age and condition, but the fabric's finish was cracked and split from years of use and wear. The rest of the room was filled with life vests, buoys, and casting nets. There was an old television set in the corner with foil-covered rabbit ear antennas. The front of the cottage was glassed in on all three sides and faced the bay with a breathtaking view of the water. This would become her favorite room. A dining table sat to the left side of the long room, and to the right were four single beds arranged head to foot around the perimeter of the room, which served to create a sleeping porch. Behind this and off to one side of the family room was the one bedroom with a queen-size bed and the cottage's only bathroom. He led her to the bedroom. But she pulled away, instead moving to sit in the glassed room watching the water, the moon, and the bay.

"But, I thought we could be alone," he said, disappointed.

"We are alone," she answered, watching the disappointment on his face fade to anticipation.

Together, they sat on a single bed that overlooked the bay. He turned her head to his and kissed her tenderly. The tenderness grew hungry, strong, and commanding. His kisses grew more passionate and demanding, filling her with an arousal that both shocked and thrilled her. He slowly pushed her down on the mattress while his hands explored the softness of her breasts through the thin white blouse she wore. Delighted and astonished, she realized that with complete ease he had unbuttoned the blouse as his fingers now danced across her stomach, neck, and breasts. His mouth moved slowly down her neck, taking time to discover every inch of skin left exposed by her open blouse. His lips returned again to hers as if time was theirs and the urgency would wait.

"I love you, you know that don't you," his blue eyes locking with hers as if he was staring into the depths of her soul. "I hope you know it's true."

Anna nodded.

"Tell me, I want to hear you say it then, tell me now," he whispered.

"I love you too," she whispered in return.

He wrapped her in his arms and held her as if to never let go. "Please let me show you then."

She understood his urgency and their hunger for each other, but guilt, fear, and all the lessons of her youth overtook her, and no was all she could think of.

"I am not ready," was her only response, knowing deep in her heart it was what she wanted too.

Through so many secret visits to the cottage over that summer, he honored her, never pushing her for more than she was ready to give. Growing ever closer still, she trusted him and never felt anything but completely safe by his side.

Chapter Two

Fifty, November 2010

ATLANTA TRAFFIC CRAWLED SLOWLY north on Interstate 75. Drivers jockeyed for position as eight lanes of traffic snaked through the city. Headlights ahead and in Anna's rearview mirror foretold of the long commute home. Although it was just mid-morning, the skies were darkened by pending thunderstorms. She hoped to make it home before the weather hit. Anna was relieved they had taken separate cars, as her husband had explained, he had to be in the office at 11:30 for a conference call. She was thankful now for time alone to understand all that had just transpired.

They had just left one of many sessions with a marriage counselor, sessions that provided little insight or answers to the problems that plagued her marriage, until today. Her hands still shook as she gripped the steering wheel. She could feel the tension running to her fingertips. She inhaled deeply and tried to calm herself.

She hated the counselor's office. Everything was beige: the walls, the furnishings, and carpet. Two small love seats were positioned in front of the counselor's desk. A small table separated them. On the table was a box of tissues and literature for various counseling opportunities. A wooden crate filled with broken toys sat in the corner of the room along with a child-size table and chair. A small window provided a view of the parking deck and most of the light in the room. Diplomas and honors hung unevenly on the wall behind the desk and a leafless plant needing water sunk in its pot beneath the window. It was such a depressing place, drained of life or joy. Anna had asked her husband for months to consider outside help in an effort to try to salvage their marriage. When he finally agreed, he sought a referral for the counselor through the Employee Assistance Program at work. He wanted the insurance program to pay—not him.

Anna sat down on one love seat, John on the other.

"I find it interesting that after several sessions, you still choose not to sit with your wife," the counselor said, peering over his glasses. "I fear you have not taken my suggestions to heart."

"Suggestions?" repeated John.

"Why yes, you were to take a weekend retreat together and concentrate on listening to each other. How did that go?" quizzed the counselor.

"Oh, that, yes. My schedule at work prevented it. So I am trying now to start planning that," he stammered.

"Anna, what was your reaction to the weekend falling through?" He turned his attention to her.

"I asked several times about planning it together. He said he would handle it. The more I asked the more bothered he became, and so I stopped," she replied.

"Stopped what?" asked the counselor.

"Stopped hoping and caring," she said. "I did not honestly expect it to happen."

"There she goes again, and I am the one who ends up in trouble!" her husband snipped.

"Trouble?" repeated the counselor.

"Yes, that is how it feels to me," said John.

"I have offered many ideas to you, John, none of which you have taken action on. Dating, without sex, as a way to get talking again. Walks, ballroom dance classes, couple's classes at church, and meeting for lunch on weekdays. All of which you seem to have no time or interest for. My suggestions were a way to open the lines of communication between you and Anna."

"She is always busy with the kids, and has no time for me," he said with a look of disgust on his face. "She pays no attention to me, I am always left out."

"So, do you join in with the kids?" asked the counselor.

"I am a great dad if that is what you are implying!" he replied with irritation in his voice.

"Why no—that's not at all what I am saying. Let me say it this way: I believe you have placed Anna in the role as your mother too. And as a result, any communication between you two is as a child to a parent. You, John, are the child and Anna the parent. Am I making myself clear?" he asked.

John sat silent.

"You claim over and over that there is no other woman in your life and that you have been a faithful husband. However, your wife is very attractive and seems full of life. You remain defensive, remote, and fail to take any action to improve your marriage. So I have come to the conclusion that you have made Anna your mother too," the counselor continued.

Anna sat stunned. He was right. Somewhere between the dirty diapers and the classroom plays, her role as wife and mother were intermingled, her womanhood lost. He caressed the remote control more than he did her. She was now *his* mother too. She had always believed he had more to offer her, their marriage, and their family, but for some reason he chose to withhold it from her. But as she sat listening to him during these sessions, it became ever so clear. There was nothing left to uncover, he had nothing to give her emotionally or he would have worked toward that goal. As an icy chill ran through her body, she realized that this was not how she wanted to live out the rest of her life. She wanted a mate, a lover, and a friend. Through the years, in her husband's eyes, she had become his mother and ceased being his wife. How and why she could not fathom, but she knew in her heart it was true. She longed for the emotional connection that led to true intimacy, but it would never be found in her marriage. Still, she craved the love and affection that eluded her all these married years. She was starved for it and terrified that she would live her life and never find it.

John hurried to the elevator, pushing past Anna in his rush out of the office. He leaped into the open elevator ahead of her, as was his style. He always went first and she was always left feeling trampled behind. No words were spoken as they descended down to ground level.

"I will call tonight when I am leaving the office," he said abruptly as he exited the elevator and hurried to his car.

Alone, Anna headed to the parking lot and to her car. She couldn't remember when she stopped caring. Perhaps it was a gradual change fueled by lack of attention and intimacy from a spouse who was never genuine from the beginning of the relationship. But she didn't care anymore and knew this was the last session they would be attending.

As she navigated the traffic homeward, she searched her memory to the early years of dating John Horton. He was attractive and quick witted. She like the way his blonde hair curled up around his face and neck with highlights touched by the sun. They only dated a few months before marriage. Anna was in her early thirties and involved heavily in her career. Most of her friends were married now and raising babies. Friends talked of kindergarten, Halloween costumes, play dates, first words, or baby's first steps. She talked of runway shows, seasonal collections, and corporate buyouts.

Something felt vacant or missing in her life. Something work could no longer fill. As she held her first-born niece for the very first time, Anna was overwhelmed with the feeling of love. It was a love she had never felt before; the love for a baby. From that day on, she was consumed with the longing for a family. She wanted a husband and a baby and the settled life that goes along with both.

John Horton entered her life. He had a good job in sales that kept him traveling. They dated, seeing each other only on weekends. They talked for hours on the phone. He was charming and kept her laughing. She never quite read what was held within his dark brown eyes, but they intrigued her, putting blinders in place when she should have looked deeper. Questions spoke softly in her mind while they were dating, but she chose to ignore them. She convinced herself that she had found a good mate and as her biological clock ticked on, she looked no further. They married and continued to pursue their respective careers, she in town and he on the road.

Anna knew on her honeymoon that she had made a mistake. But she decided to keep her concerns to herself, hidden away. He was under tremendous stress at work, that must be the reason, she rationalized. She did all she could to be supportive, attractive, and positive. He blamed her; it was her fault. He had never had trouble performing while they were dating or before with other women, he liked to emphasize. Trying not to put him under more stress, she stayed optimistic. Anna reasoned with herself to be patient and loving, he would open up to her soon. Still, she got excuses and distance instead. Sex was sporadic at best, always rushed, leaving her empty and unfulfilled. She had believed he had more to offer, but for some reason he chose to withhold it from her. Yet, Anna learned early in her marriage, he could not give what he never had or felt.

Through the years, she found herself foregoing the authentic love and life she so desperately craved. She longed for the emotional connection that led to true intimacy, but it would never be found in her marriage. The counselor made this evident today, although deep in her heart she already knew it to be true.

The rain came with a fury as Anna pulled into her driveway. Her windshield wipers could not keep up with the wind-fueled rain. She waited as the garage door opened and watched leaves and twigs swirling in the wind and rain.

She dropped her keys and purse on the kitchen table and went to the computer to check her email. The desktop was open to an unfamiliar email page. A pain stabbed her heart as she read.

"The darkness of this stormy night is only brightened by knowing I will see you tomorrow for lunch. I will call you when I get to the office," his words sprang from the computer screen. He signed off simply "J". The email thread continued back for days as she read on until she could stomach no more. She closed the computer and felt numb, nothingness. There were no tears, nothing.

"How long and how could I have been so stupid?" she said out loud to the small black dog at her feet. "So this is how it feels to be made the fool."

She wondered how she had gotten this far, ignoring the many warning signs. Perhaps she was too focused on her two children, the grocery list, the laundry, keeping the appointments, and paying bills. She was always able to give love and find joy in her children, while ignoring the crumbling marriage that had turned into separate bedrooms and no conversation. Her joy was her children and living in them. But now they were rightly becoming independent and finding their own place in life.

Anna walked to her bedroom and pulled a suitcase from the closet, putting it on her bed. She was intent on escaping for a while. She needed time alone to reflect on where the unraveling began and how the seams of her life had become split and torn. She needed time to think. Clarity was what she sought and there was one place to go that still called out to her heart and soul.

She caught her reflection in the large mirror on her dresser. There stood a woman, age fifty, unloved and cheated on. She saw such sadness in her face. The sadness had been there for some time, but she failed to recognize it until now. She looked tired, joyless, and drained. She wondered about the boy she once loved. Would he still find her attractive? Does he ever think of her and would he still want her? No one had for so long. She doubted herself and fought to hold back her tears. Would he be different or still find her as he once did, lovely and desirable?

She turned away from her reflection and looked at the open suitcase. Knowing she had to face her husband later that evening, Anna decided to leave in the morning. As she packed her clothes, she tried to prepare her words for the confrontation that loomed ahead. It would not be easy, but at least she now knew the truth. Having no answers and blaming herself did nothing but undermine her spirit. Now she knew. She prayed for strength as she finished packing and waited for John to come home.

Her children understood as she explained later that afternoon. She needed to go away for a few days. An old friend from Mobile had called and needed her help. She was sorry for the short notice, but so hoped I could come, she told Will and Carrie. Keeping to herself, the old friend needing help, was indeed her own lost and wounded soul.

"How long will you be gone, Mom?" her son Will, now seventeen, asked.

"I will be home on Saturday, five days should be enough time," Anna replied.

"I promise I will take care of Carrie, Mom. We will be fine. Dad will be here too, so go, we will be great."

Carrie was a bit more reluctant.

"Can I come too, Mom?" asked her thirteen-year-old daughter, her dark eyes welling with tears.

"Oh, my dear, no tears," Anna said. "I need to go and help my friend. You will be fine here with Will and Dad. I promise to call you and you can call or text me anytime. But Carrie, I need to do this."

Anna comforted her daughter, holding her close in embrace, stroking her long black hair.

"I love you both more than anything, you know that too. This will just be a few days," Anna said as she pulled her son into the embrace as well.

Once her children understood her decision, Anna told them she would not leave until the morning when they both left for school. Will was driving now and enjoyed taking his sister to school. Carrie felt quite grown-up riding with her big brother.

That evening, as she waited for John to come home, she decided. It was a divorce she wanted. No more pretend fixes this time, instead, her freedom.

Chapter Three

Endless Summer, 1978

AS SHE CROSSED THE GEORGIA STATE LINE into Alabama, Anna realized she had not called ahead and so had no reservations and no place to say. It was November; surely there would be vacancies. She would work all that out when she arrived. Earlier that morning she promised her children, as they left for school, that she would be home on Saturday. She kissed them each good-bye, waved them off, got in her car, and starting driving south.

Interstate 75 stretched for miles, turning into hours of personal reflection before emptying into Interstate 65 and leading her farther south. She passed the Auburn University exit signs and smiled, remembering her college days and how the Alabama football team had been a staunch Auburn rival. She was tempted to turn off and ride through the campus. Long ago, she and a few college friends had gone on a road trip to attend the Alabama and Auburn game, which the Crimson Tide, of course, won. Those youthful times were just memories now and she was focused on returning to the Gulf of Mexico. Along with the passing miles, her mind began to wander back to her summers of years long gone. Happier times, times filled with excitement, love, and youthful exuberance. The years she lived on the Gulf Coast. She smiled as her mind drifted back to the summer of 1978 through the hypnotic hum of the interstate below.

They were inseparable and completely lost in each other. They spent their days taking classes and working, seizing any chance to escape to Gulf Shores across the bay. The sleepy beach town at the end of Highway 59 was littered with family vacation homes built on stilts and pilings. Some were painted yellow, others white, and many were gray, weathered from years of sun and sea salt air. Porches wrapped around the houses, providing views of the water. Hammocks swung in the breeze while Alabama, Auburn, Georgia, and Tennessee college flags flew proudly, staking their claims over the dwellings while declaring the owner's unwavering loyalties. This yet undiscovered town was the vacationland for the wealthy families of Mobile, Birmingham, Montgomery, New Orleans, Atlanta, and Nashville. Houses hidden in the dunes of the sugar-white sand were mostly vacant except those peak months of June, July, and August. By September, it was a ghost town as families returned home to pursue work as bankers, doctors, lawyers, and stockbrokers. College-aged sons and daughters returned to campus, dreaming of spring breaks to come, and younger siblings returned to classrooms across the South.

At the end of the highway and water's edge was a boardwalk of tacky bars, shell and T-shirt shops, the public beach, and washhouse. This beach was always crowded during the summer months with the residents of Baldwin and Mobile counties who couldn't afford a summer home but came for the beer, the sun, and the promise of love among the multitude of girls that bounced in the waves in halter tops and bikinis, hoping to be noticed. Boys in cut-off jeans and surfer shorts tossed footballs across the sand while trying to look casual as they surveyed the beauties before them—deciding on which ones to focus their attention. Radios blared, all turned to different FM stations, some rock and some country, but all playing Lynyrd Skynyrd's "Freebird" or "Sweet Home Alabama."

Heading east toward Orange Beach, past the state park picnic areas, there was nothing but family beach homes built on pilings on both sides of the two-lane highway, and the yellow shell of an old single story motel washed out by a long-forgotten hurricane. Sometimes, during that first summer, they would park on the side of the road, walk over the dunes, and spread out their blankets across the sugar-white sand. If anyone came into sight, they would move farther down the beach. Just beyond Orange Beach were the jetties of Perdido

Key. Though beautiful, the currents were too swift to enjoy the surf and fishing. The Florida state line and the Flora-Bama lounge were just ahead.

Anna recalled the first time he took her there. She had spent several weekends in Gulf Shores with her family the previous summer before they met. But he had somewhere special he wanted to show her.

He packed his car with towels, a beach blanket, a cooler with drinks, and his crab net, a long wooden stick with a net on the end. It reminded Anna of a butterfly net. She brought sandwiches and a bag of chips, which they opened and ate while they drove. They listened to his favorite band, Boston, on the eight-track tape player in his car on the way over the bay, singing along with the tape. The warm June air blew through the open windows.

"This beach I want to show you is special," he said as he turned right on Fort Morgan Road, rather than follow the main road into Gulf Shores.

"I promise you will love it. It's just a bit longer ride—but so worth it."

Fort Morgan was a twenty-minute drive west of Gulf Shores. He was right, it became her favorite beach too. The old Civil War fort sat at the westernmost point of the peninsula, and just before entering the historic grounds, a road headed off to the left and ended at the dunes of the Gulf. Rarely would they see anyone on this road, and the beach provided complete privacy. There were no homes, there were no condos, and there were no people.

He parked his car and found a spot to place the blanket, towels, and picnic basket.

"Let's go," he said as he grabbed her hand and led her up the beach to the point where the old fort stood watch over the waters it guarded. He had a small cooler in one hand and a crab net in the other.

"There's one!" he shouted with excitement as he dashed along the shore to pluck the crab from the waters and dropping it into his cooler.

She laughed at his ritual dance, splashing through the waves, as he gathered more crabs to feast on later in the evening when the sting of the day's sun would continue to warm their skin.

The point at which Mobile Bay met the Gulf of Mexico always provided the best catch of crabs. Sometimes if he was quick enough, a tasty flounder was captured in his net, adding to his delight. An occasional nurse shark was caught and immediately released. He worried its sharp teeth would do damage to his crab net.

On the water out before them, shrimp boats trolled back and forth in front of the fort, filling their nets with the pink delicacy. Their motors hummed as seagulls flew shrieking above the vessels, then diving into the waters to catch the shrimp too small to be snared by the nets. Blue heron and pelicans stood on the water's edge as white sandpipers scampered along the surf gathering winnows. This was the music of his beach, their beach.

On occasion, that summer, they shared their beach with friends or family, but mostly they enjoyed the hidden discovery alone. They would lie on a blanket beneath the Alabama sun, slowly and deliberately rub each other's body with cocoa tanning butter until their skin glistened, cool off in the surf, and walk the beach in search of the evening's meal.

Later in the evening, he taught her how to cook and crack the blue crab that was the bounty of their day at the beach. They would spread old newspaper across the long dining table and pour the steaming crabs out on to the center of the table. Using a small wooden mallet and a knife was his way to split the claws to get at the sweet meat inside. He patiently worked at cleaning his crabs and making a huge pile of crabmeat on his plate before he would take the time to eat it. She would immediately eat each morsel of crabmeat she extracted from the shell, only to try to invade his plate and steal the efforts of his hard work. He laughed and guarded his plate, pretending to be annoyed, but always let her take whatever she wanted. When they were visiting the secret cottage, they would clean up as if no one had been there. After the meal they would spend hours on the sleeping cots, holding onto each other, discovering what pleasured them both, always stopping before they had gone too far.

Sometimes they would return to her home from the beach trips and share the day's catch with her family, spending the evenings together in her parents' home watching late-night television and doing what they could to enjoy and discover each other. They were ever mindful that at any moment they might be interrupted, as she was under the watchful eye of her mother. Her parents were known to appear unannounced just to be sure her conduct was without question.

As she drove south, Anna recalled one night in particular and to this day still did not understand why what they were doing was wrong. They were watching television when her parents said good night and left the room. Seeing his chance to finally be close to her, he dove across the sofa on top of her in embrace. At that very moment, her mother reentered the room.

"Anna, I want to see you in the kitchen immediately, and tell your young man good night now," her mother said as she passed through the room.

Anna did as instructed, and he left.

"You must always conduct yourself as a young lady," her mother told Anna, trying to control her anger. "What I just saw is not such behavior. Boys are only interested in sex and once you give into them, they will never marry you. Your reputation will be ruined, and then no one will want you."

"But, I didn't do anything, he simply came over to hug me," Anna protested.

"That's not what I saw! Passion is a dangerous thing and once it takes hold, you lose all control and find yourself in a place where you cannot turn back. That young man is passionate when it comes to you. You must always act like a lady. A man who loves you will protect you and honor your commitment to remaining chaste as a bride," her mother further continued.

"He loves me and would never do anything to hurt me," Anna replied.

"Mind my words," her mother added. "You must be careful and responsible and keep your options open for the future. Who knows, you may meet a doctor or lawyer one day, a young lady would certainly want to save herself for that kind of man."

Anna was stunned as she obediently went to her room. What she just heard could not be true. She never felt anything but completely natural, safe, and loved when she was with him. He had no reason to demand or force her to have sex before she was ready and then leave her unequipped to suffer whatever consequences would follow. He was happy to just be with her and understood what she was ready to do and never pushed or demanded more. He had proved his patience already. She was just nineteen and trying to discover herself slowly. He was fine with that. And so as these sermons were frequently thrust upon her, she found them unnecessary. What she found most annoying in these lectures was how once the ring was placed on one's finger, sex suddenly became a beautiful and wonderful expression between husband and wife. The shackles were removed as quickly as the bonds of matrimony were sealed and happiness and wedded bliss erased all the evils of premarital relations. Sex was scorned without the marriage bond and instantly blissful once the wedding ceremony was completed. So went the many lectures that followed, senseless as they seemed to Anna.

Her parents attempted to break into the social fiber of their new community and found they were welcomed at first. Invitations to parties and coveted Mardi Gras balls were presented through the bankers and lawyers working with her father in building the manufacturing facility he was brought to town to oversee. They were Northerners, who were courted to an extent, as the business relationships of the new facility were being forged. As long as he placed his business with the most prominent bank in town, employed the oldest, most respected law firms, and hired the sons of the well-heeled, the courtship continued.

Mardi Gras was the culmination of all of the social events of the year. A whirlwind of luncheons, teas, dinner galas, parades, and balls swirled through the weeks leading up to that one festive day.

The most prestigious of these gala events were scheduled the closest to Mardi Gras and were hosted by the upper echelons of society. Invitations to these dinners, posh parties, and balls were much harder to garner. Members of the secret societies hosting these coveted parties were given a limited number of invitations to share with family and friends. During their first few years in town, her parents were asked to attend the best parties and balls, but once business relationships were established and accounts in place, these invitations dwindled. Her mother tried to push Anna into friendships with the children of these local prominent businessmen, and for a time she was included because of her parents. Her beauty further opened these doors. She mingled with the debutantes and their beaus, who reigned as the queens, kings, knights, ladies in waiting, and pages of the royal courts of Mardi Gras. Children with Southern pedigrees, extending back decades through their parents and grandparents, a tapestry rich in tradition, pageantry, and local history. When Ash Wednesday arrived, all gaiety and frivolity ceased. It was then the month's-long celebrations, feasts, and public drunkenness turned to sober and proper behavior. The once-masked revelers could suddenly be found drying out in church pews and confessional booths.

Anna wanted to please her parents so she accepted the invitations that came her way. She tried to fit in and understand the close-knit hierarchy of this old Southern town, but felt the alienation of not having grown up there. She had not gone to the private schools, the etiquette classes, or the ballroom lessons, and clearly felt ill at ease. Dashing her parents' hopes, she focused on her boyfriend, growing less interested in social pursuits. But they continued to direct her to set her sights for a man of prominence. Although her boyfriend's family had deep roots in the city, they were not of the upper class—not from wealth or descendants of the leading prominent families. And so she wondered, did her parents approve of him, the relationship, and the obvious love they had for each other? She was guilty of nothing and unimpressed by the children of society, and so she dismissed their direction, and gave all of her attention to him.

* * *

The water defined him and made him who he was. He loved being part of the vast estuary that was the Mobile

Bay leading down to the Gulf of Mexico. He would take the blue boat out at any chance he could to the waters that always beckoned him. With her by his side, they explored the bayous and inlets of Dog River, Rabbit Creek, Mobile Bay, and beyond. From wandering the musky alligator-infested corners of creeks to water skiing the wide bends of Dog River, this was his home.

He kept the blue boat at his uncle's waterfront home on Dog River. He and his brother had saved their money together to make this purchase. And together they built a covered boatlift on the family dock to house their boat. It was here she first met his family. It started with his cousins and their girlfriends spending weekends on the boat, water skiing, and tubing out on the river. Friends and their dates soon joined in. Their fun and accessibility to the bay, river, and water sports was determined by his endless generosity, to the point that, at times, she felt he was being used. He just laughed off her concern, as was his natural giving spirit. Until one Saturday's trip across the bay to ski the cool spring fed waters of Magnolia Springs.

Two of his friends from high school and their girlfriends sat in the back of the boat, Anna by her love's side. His friends drank beer, smoked cigarettes, and smeared baby oil over their legs. Cackles of laughter rose from the girls who made fun of Anna's accent as she talked. She said "Golf" of Mexico instead of "Gulf" of Mexico, and "dog" instead of "dawg," and "getting ready" instead of "fixin' to."

They laughed as Anna fell time and time again, trying to rise out of the water on two skis. He patiently floated beside her in the water trying to help her stand, as his friend hit the throttle to pull her up. With each fall, the laughter increased. Irritation crept slowly across his face.

As he helped Anna up the ladder and back into the boat, the girls commented on her red bathing suit: a one-piece halter as was the style in 1978.

"Did you borrow my mom's bathing suit?" one guest asked Anna.

"No," giggled her friend. "See the gathers on the top, she needs those because clearly there is nothing else there."

They both donned string bikinis and had curves that spilled out over their tops.

Thin like a dancer, Anna looked down on her own chest, turning to him to see his reaction. He was stoned faced.

"What did you say?" his eyes darting from one girl to the other.

"Nothing, nothing at all!" one guest responded before turning to her friend saying, "Let's jump in." Over the side of the boat both girls jumped, splashing all left behind.

"This is the last time they will be invited on my boat," he turned and said to his friends—their dates.

"Come on," one friend replied. "You know that they are just jealous and mad that you are dating Anna now and not Pam."

"Pam?" Anna asked.

"They are friends with someone I went out with a few times last year," he said softly.

"Dumped," belted the other friend. "You dumped her as fast as you could for Anna, and you know it."

"None of that matters now, Anna is with me!" he said with great irritation. "Tell them to get in the boat, we are going back."

Clouds gathered overhead covering the sun. Anna pulled on her shorts and a T-shirt while trying to ignore the glares from the two girls drying off in the back of the boat. She instead watched him as he pulled in the ski ropes. He kept looking at the darkening sky.

He became a madman racing across the bay. Determined to beat the approaching thunderstorms, the boat leaped across the small white caps kicked up by the growing wind. He could tell she was terrified, clutching the boat seat in fear. He pulled the throttle back to slow the boat from crashing down on the waves, ever mindful of the nearing storm ahead of them. His hair was wild from the blowing wind and his eyes, full of determination, reflected the steel blue of the water surrounding them. Through her fear she saw how the bay inspired him. He loved the spray of the water, the sound of the raging seagulls, the boom of the thunder above, and the unfaltering command of his ship.

She grew to like his older cousin's girlfriend and soon-to-be fiancé, so much so that boat trips and skiing almost always included them. On occasional weekend nights that summer, they would double date, going to Pensacola's Seville Quarter to drink hurricanes and dance. It was the era of disco and the beat of the music shook the restaurants, bars, and dance floors across the lower south. Phineas Phogg's, with its two levels of dance floors, was the premium club along the Gulf Coast, and Florida's legal drinking age of eighteen helped attract college students from neighboring Alabama. Mirror balls sent shimmering light and glitter over the sweating bodies that danced below. But even among the disco songs, "Firebird" and "Sweet Home Alabama"—the anthems of summer—found their way into the disc jockey's mix. The patrons reacted to these songs with such joy, spilling onto the lighted dance floor, to emphasize the love and pride they felt for the South, their home—a love she would come to understand and from which she would never waver.

Anna recalled one Saturday night in August when both couples were sitting in the courtyard of the Seville Quarter waiting for dinner to be served. A waitress, carrying a tray of hurricanes to a nearby table, slipped, losing control of her tray. The flaming drinks caught her long, loose hair on fire and in her panic the tray crashed to the ground, spilling the drinks on customers seated nearby. Her boyfriend saw the flames and rushed to extinguish them from the waitress's hair using his hands, a linen napkin, and his water glass. His reaction was so swift—the flames were out before anyone had time to realize what had happened. The waitress was in tears and threw her arms around him in thanks. By then the restaurant management had gathered and were cleaning up around them, making apologies to all affected.

Within minutes, they were led to another table and told that the meal and drinks were complimentary. Almost immediately, a tray of hurricanes arrived at their table as an additional thank you before the meal was served. The drinks were potent and Anna could not finish hers. He drank his and hers. Fried shrimp and fried crab craws, baked potatoes, and coleslaw were brought to the table before any of them had time to survey the menu. Once dinner was complete, they walked through the complex following the sound of bass and treble to the disco club, Phineas Phogg's, where they danced the evening away.

By midnight it was time to return to Mobile, a forty-five minute drive west. She was already late for her curfew and knew her parents would be waiting. The night was foggy and the roads were dark. Highway 98 was undergoing construction work and the detour signs were poorly marked, leading them to drive in the wrong direction. Miles passed as signs for Fort Walton were clearly in the distance and he swore under his breath. They were driving in the opposite direction from home. He pulled off the road into a 7-Eleven convenience market, pulling a map from his glove box.

"Let me take over driving," his cousin said from the backseat. "I know where we are."

Anna slipped into the backseat and he handed the keys to his cousin, the more sober of the two, before climbing in next to her.

"I am so scared, what will my parents say?" she whispered to him. Looking at his watch, it was 1:15.

"We can stop and call them," he said.

"No, maybe they will be asleep and not know what time I get in."

He heard the concern in her voice and worried too, he knew they watched her closely. He was afraid that they would prevent him from seeing her if he did not honor their rules. So with each passing mile they both grew more nervous, checking his wristwatch constantly. He buried his head in her shoulder and as the liquor took over, his emotions were revealed.

"They can't keep you from me, Anna, if you are late," he whispered, his voice cracking.

Anna felt his tears on her neck.

"I'd die without you, they can't keep me from you," his voice trailing off through his tears.

"They won't, I won't let them, I promise," she said, trying to soothe him as they approached Mobile. He buried his head in her lap and cried. She ran her hands over his back and curled his brown hair around her fingers, trying to reassure him that it would be all right.

Shortly before three a.m. they pulled into her driveway and all the lights were on in the house.

The front door flew open and her mother appeared.

"Where have you been, don't you know we have been sick with worry?"

"We got lost—there was construction and the detours were misleading," Anna tried to explain.

"Get in this house now!" demanded her mother and then directing her comments to him, she added, "We trusted you with our daughter, how am I to trust you again?"

"It's true, Ma'am, we were lost and somehow ended up headed to Fort Walton Beach," he said.

"Well, you should have called then," her mother said. "Wouldn't that have been the thing to do? Have you no judgment?"

"Yes, Ma'am, I should have called you, I am so sorry, I promise it will never happen again," he said, almost pleading.

"You are correct, it will not happen again. Good night," she said, closing the door.

Once inside, Anna was left wondering just what her mother meant.

"It's time for you to take a break from that boy, you are too young for this relationship," her mother said.

"But he loves me," Anna said softly.

"Go to bed, we will discuss this in the morning."

Chapter Four

AS SUMMER ENDED AND CLASSES RESUMED, he tried to arrange his schedule to see her as much as he could, even if it meant running to an adjacent building just to kiss her during a break between classes. He had honored the "few weeks away from each other" imposed by her parents and was thrilled that class was again in session so he could she her more often. She spent most of her time in the Humanities Building, he in the Engineering Building on the opposite side of the campus. But he always managed to see her at least once during the day to hug her or kiss her or just spend a precious moment with her. They waited for each other in the parking lot when their classes were over. He would wrap her in his arms, commenting on how she was made just for him. He was just over six feet tall and she was five feet six inches, so as he would pull her in to him to hold her closely, she fit just under his arms and he always said she was the "perfect fit."

One Friday night that September, he arranged to pick her up after work as he was still working his way back into her parents' graces. There were no special plans, or so she thought. He waited outside the dress shop where she worked, sitting on a mall bench in front of the store. He was wearing jeans and her favorite steel blue shirt. She loved the way it complemented his eyes and dark hair.

She locked the doors to the dress shop and waved good night to her co-worker. He stood up to greet her, throwing his arms around her shoulders as he always did. Once again he whispered, "You fit me perfectly."

They headed to the parking lot, he opened his car door for her, sliding in beside her and closing the door. He leaned over and kissed her with such determination it surprised her. He produced a handwritten note, in blue pen and on three-ring-binder college-ruled paper, which was folded over twice.

"Read it," he said excitedly, "I wrote it just for you."

Though simple in presentation, it was not in meaning and Anna's eyes filled with tears as she read the heartfelt poem:

> There is nothing I can do today,
> The only words I know to say,
> Are one day soon, I will make you mine;
> And love you to the end of time.

> But for now, I hope you know,
> The love I have will always grow.
> It's in the things I say and do,
> I love you, Anna. I love you true.

He next produced a black velvet box that he couldn't wait to give her. Surprised and questioning, she looked at him through tears she was unable to hold back, touched by the sweet sincerity of the poem.

"Open it," he said excitedly.

In it she found a necklace made of coral, carved in the shape of a small fish. She had seen the necklace a few days earlier. They had gone shopping together after classes to find some new clothes for him. Clothes he really needed. He had asked for her input on styles and colors, mostly he wanted to look nice for her. While walking through D. H. Holmes department store, he had steered her to the jewelry department and showed her a display of treasures from the sea, including a starfish dipped in gold, and all manner of coral pieces framed in earrings, rings, and bracelets. He pointed to a little white fish that hung from a delicate gold chain. She loved it and agreed that he had great taste in discovering things to do with fishing and the sea, his real true love she said. They laughed as he hugged her and thanked her for understanding that the water was indeed his first love, before heading off in search of the men's department.

Anna stared at the open box and little coral fish, knowing that his paycheck and savings had gone to pay for this necklace, instead of the clothes he so needed. But he didn't care. He knew she loved him regardless of what he wore, and he wanted her to know she mattered most in his life.

"I want you to wear this and remember the wonderful summer we spent together, our first of many summers," he whispered in her ear as he draped the necklace around her neck and hooked the clasp.

Thirty years later, the little fish necklace remained one of her most prized possessions, for it immortalized the purity of the love and devotion they gave each other. Tucked away safely in her jewelry box, Anna kept it all these years, only to take it out on occasion to feel the deep emotion it invoked in her still.

Her grades during her freshman year were average at best. Now a sophomore, she was enrolled in algebra for the second time, having failed miserably the first time through. He tried his best to tutor her, even secretly sending her the test answers as he sat behind her during her first attempt at the college course. Still undecided on a major, her parents began applying pressure for improvement. They expected their children to graduate from college. It was the means to a good life. You must be able to take care of yourself and provide for your family should anything ever happen to your spouse, they reasoned. She should be more focused on her studies and not her boyfriend. If he truly loved her he would wait. She should concentrate on her studies, perhaps at another university where she could pursue her goals and focus on a career path. The chances of meeting a husband of great potential also came with a college degree. Once she was established in a career, she would have time to look for a husband. They didn't have to add, a more suitable husband.

Periodically, she toyed with the idea of going away. She was curious about the college experiences she was missing, having forgone her acceptance to Purdue University to move to the South. She was still living at home with her family. High school friends wrote her letters about their adventures in dormitory life, with stories of crazy roommates, sorority rush, fraternity parties with rock bands, football weekends, and independence. She regretted missing the opportunity to sample firsthand the experiences college life in another town would bring. But, she loved her boyfriend and could not imagine leaving him. When a work friend, Caroline, approached her about transferring to the University of Alabama with her, a pang of regret stabbed her heart for the experiences that might be lost forever. It was time to apply for the next semester and the chance would not come around again for six months if she did not take it. She promised to consider the move with an open mind; meanwhile, time was passing on.

His family had hoped for a Catholic girl for their son. His mother worried that he was not attending Mass and confession, as he should. He was indifferent to the idea. Years in the Catholic school system left him yearning for freedom from what he saw as an unnecessary task. Each and every Sunday, his mother reminded him that it was time to go to Mass. Usually he went to the grocery store where he worked instead, and called her from the payphone on the outside of the building. He hated being told to do anything, especially confession, and he made every effort to avoid this particular chore. But his mother pleaded weekly with her son and reminded him that church was the place to meet nice Catholic girls.

In early October, she met his parents for the first time. They hosted a gathering at the family cottage— their secret cottage. Pretending never to have been there before proved amusing to her and he delighted in trying to trip her up. His parents had no idea that he had had a key made to the cottage. Pleasantries and small talk were the order of the afternoon. When she asked to help in the kitchen, his mother replied, "Oh no, Amy, you are our guest."

Anna smiled and corrected her as respectfully as she could, "It's Anna," she said softly.

"Yes, dear, I am sorry," his mother replied, focused on putting a casserole in the oven, before pulling paper plates from a grocery bag.

"Let me take those for you," Anna offered, as his mother continued about the kitchen.

"Where did you say you graduated from, Amy?" asked his mother.

"I went to high school in Indiana," she replied.

"Yes, of course, I remember you are not from the South, your accent is interesting, Indiana, you say. Was this a

Catholic high school?" she probed further, knowing in fact that her son's girlfriend was not a Catholic.

"No, Ma'am, I went to a public high school," Anna answered. "Can I help you set the table?"

"No, no, we have everything under control, Amy," his mother said, waving her hand in the air.

Anna backed out of the kitchen feeling as though the impression she had made was not a good one. Not wanting to correct her hostess again, Anna answered to Amy the rest of the evening. She joined him out in front of the cottage where he was working on detangling fishing lines and getting the casting nets ready for night fishing.

"Your mom keeps calling me Amy," she said. "I don't think she likes me."

"Of course she does, how could she not, you are so wonderful." Looking up at her from his work he added, "I love you."

She smiled, watching him so earnest in his work. She wanted him to know how uncomfortable she was, but he missed these signs in his excitement to show her off to his family. Anna chose to let it drop and joined in to help him with the nets. Her arm brushed against his and she felt her heart stir, sending an erotic sensation through her body, something she tried so hard to ignore when parents were nearby. So she leaned to kiss him, to which he quickly responded. That was enough, for now.

During the fall semester she worked hard to improve her grades and tried to find relevance in the courses she found so boring. Pre-calculus, philosophy, and sociology were painfully difficult to find of interest. She wanted to explore colors, fabrics, and expand on the fashion designs she doodled in the margins of her notebooks when she should have been taking class notes. He helped her as much as he could. But the concentration level suffered as neither were able to keep their hands off each other and the work went undone. So these study sessions had to end. The class load he was carrying, and the work required of a second-year engineering student, kept him focused on the goal of graduation. He was still working a part-time job and juggling the demands of that made his study time precious. He paid for his courses through his job and student loans. Any course he might fail was lost money and would only set him back financially and keep him in school longer. He was determined to get out and go to work at one of the many new industrial complexes that had moved into the area.

Never able to stay apart for long, they still found time together, movies and school dances at the old Brookley Officer's Club or on the weekend evenings at the cottage if he wasn't working.

"Make sure you get off work on November sixth," he reminded her for weeks leading up to the date.

Anna smiled and promised she would.

He picked her up that Saturday and headed down to the bay and their secret cottage.

"Wait here for a minute," he said, leaving her on the back steps. "I have to fix something." Running inside for just a few minutes, he returned, his face alight with excitement. Reaching for her hand, he pulled her up the steps into the cottage, leading her to the large glassed-in room. A large mason jar of freshly picked flowers was the table's centerpiece and candles of all shapes and sizes adorned the table. Candles also flickered in windows around the perimeter of the room in smaller mason canning jars. He had run ahead to light each candle, sending soft light into the room as the sun disappeared from the day.

"It's been one year since our first date," he told her, but she already knew. "You have made me so happy this year, so tonight we are going to celebrate."

He poured her a glass of wine and opened a bottle of beer. At nineteen, he was of legal age to purchase liquor in Alabama, although he rarely did.

He clinked his bottle to her glass and laughed, "Next year will be even better!"

He set about the kitchen preparing dinner. Anna offered to help, but he would not allow her.

"This is a very special dinner, Anna," he laughed. "Not sure it's the most balanced of the food groups, but I have remembered to include all your favorites."

She smiled at his excitement and wondered what he was up to.

Anna sat in a chair off the kitchen, talking to him while he worked, but he did not want her to see the meal until it was served.

She smelled mushrooms and tried to guess what he was preparing. The smell of butter and wine cooking quickly took to the air. She sipped her wine and took great amusement in watching him.

"It's ready," he announced. Leading her to the dinner table, he pulled out her chair as she sat. Arranging the mason jar of flowers first so she could see them in all their beauty, he then disappeared into the kitchen. He carried the wine bottle and a newly opened beer, placing them on the table. Back to the kitchen, he then returned with two steaming plates. Beaming from ear to ear, he placed the meal in front of Anna.

Lump crabmeat, large shrimp, and whole mushroom caps were sautéed in a butter wine sauce. Anna detected a hint of garlic. He hurried back to the kitchen once again to retrieve a long loaf of warm French bread wrapped in foil.

"Taste it," he smiled as he sat down next her, but she did not need encouragement as she filled her fork.

He broke a piece of French bread and dipped it in his plate, absorbing some of the liquid and handed it to Anna. "Try it on the bread."

Anna did as instructed. The sauce he created was delicious but light enough not to overpower the delicate favor of the fresh lump crabmeat and shrimp. They ate until they could eat no more.

The November air was still moist as always on the waterfront, but tonight the unheated cottage had taken on an unfamiliar chill. She shivered as she cleared the table. He sent her to the porch and got her a blanket, joining her after he cleaned up the remains of the meal. They sat together under the blanket watching the remaining candles not yet burnt out flicker in the otherwise dark room. He reached beneath the small sofa, producing a small black box. Turning to her to present the package, he beamed with pride and joy. Anna opened the box and found inside a delicate gold watch. He had had her initials and the date, November 6, 1977, engraved on the back of the watch face, forever preserving the memory of their first date together.

"This is the first of many anniversaries," he whispered, his warm breath tickling her ear.

He held her as closely as he ever had, and began kissing her face and neck and then seeking out her mouth. His kisses reached into the depths of her soul, never again to be duplicated, but always longed for. His hands began to stroke across her body, as she so loved. With ease, he removed her clothes and his. Lying there, feeling the warmth of his skin on hers as he held her was the greatest sexual experience of her young life.

Chapter Five

A Beginning and an End

AS THE NEW YEAR RANG IN they danced to "Color My World" and kissed a seemly never-ending kiss at midnight. The local bar, One Nostalgia Place, on Dauphin Street was packed with revelers, but they could have been the only ones on the crowded dance floor, so lost in each other and the promise of another year together. Unknown at the time was the sadness the year's end would bring.

February brought the citywide celebration of Mardi Gras into full swing. Parades, balls, and parties continued for weeks leading up to Fat Tuesday. He invited her to come downtown with him and spend Saturday watching the parades and then attend the Mystics of Time Ball later that evening. His cousin had secured a hotel room in the Admiral Semmes Hotel and they set out to spend the day on the streets of Mobile. The day was sunny and warm for mid-February. The city streets were crowded with people following the parades, listening to the bands at different music venues playing all over downtown, and enjoying the party that was Mardi Gras. Street vendors peddled their wares and food and drink vendors were set up on every corner. Beer and alcohol flowed as the police officers and security guards looked away. This was the last weekend of endless partying, a tradition in southern Alabama.

Parades rolled through the streets as members of the secret societies riding the floats tossed bead necklaces, trinkets, candy, and Moon Pies to the crowds gathered along the sidelines. High school marching bands played and danced through the streets following the floats, creating the soundtrack for the day. Together they enjoyed the merriment of the parades and the spectacle of people watching before deciding to walk to Bienville Square at Dauphin and North Conception streets to listen to a band and find a place to sit behind the live oak trees and eat lunch. Taking a shortcut up a side street from Government Street toward the square and park, they encountered a group of three or four drunken young men in their late teens that were walking toward them and not yielding any sidewalk at all. As they passed, one of the drunks reached his hand out and let it graze across her breasts. Her boyfriend reacted with a fury she had not seen from him, grabbing the drunken youth by his shirt collar until his legs dangled in the air and then threw him on the ground. One friend came to his rescue and the friend was sent flying with a punch to the left side of his face.

"No one touches her ever, no one!" he yelled at the shocked and hurting gang who scampered away as quickly as they could. He shook his smarting hand that had delivered the powerful punch, inspecting it to make sure he had not injured himself. Then he turned to her, apologizing profusely for not protecting her. He wrapped his arm around her, pulling her as close to him as he could and they set out walking again. He buried his face in her hair and whispered over and over, "I am so sorry, babe, so sorry."

She took his hand and inspected it, making sure it was not swelling.

"I am fine," she promised him and added in her forgiving way, "It's Mardi Gras, and they were drunk. Are you okay, should we get some ice for your hand?"

"No, it's okay, let's go find something to eat for lunch and forget this even happened," he said, wrapping his arm over her shoulder as they walked.

As evening closed in, they headed back to the hotel to change. He and his cousin went downstairs to the bar and allowed the girls to shower and get ready in the hotel room. Mardi Gras balls were formal affairs and much time was spent on hair and makeup before they slipped into their evening gowns. Anna wore a white dress that was draped across one shoulder leaving the other bare, reminiscent of a Grecian gown. Silver-beaded trim cascaded down the front of the dress and decorated the one shoulder strap. She had spent hours drawing up the design and figuring out the needed yardage, before purchasing the fabric and beaded trim. Anna spent weeks creating the dress but was quite pleased with the result. She had sewn for years, a hobby passed down from her grandmother, to her mother, and now to Anna. The beaded trim proved to be the biggest challenge, so Anna sewed it on by hand. His cousin's fiancé's gown was a red halter dress with brilliant sequins draping the bodice and scattering randomly down around her hips and the length of the dress. The girls waited in the room while the men took turns showering and changing in the bathroom. With the finishing touches on the men's tuxedo cummerbunds and bowties made, they headed down to the hotel restaurant for dinner.

After the meal, they set out to the viewing stands in front of the hotel, a benefit for the paying customers of the hotel and available by ticket only. These raised platforms gave a better view of the parade and also provided seating that Anna welcomed, as she was not used to walking or standing at length in high heels. The viewing platforms also allowed the elite members of society and the family members of the krewes, or secret societies, riding in the evening's parade, protection from the masses of partygoers roaming the streets of Mobile. Those dressed in expensive evening gowns were guaranteed protected viewing of the parade while waiting for the gala ball that followed the parade's end.

Mardi Gras parades took on a different atmosphere as they rolled through the nighttime streets of Mobile. The darkened night sky and the ever-present haze cast an eerie or spooky feeling over the frivolity, different from the sun-filled day. The colorful floats lit up the night as the members of the krewe rode off into the night. The brilliant colors and style of the costumes they wore varied depending on the theme of the float. Some floats were dolphins, pirate ships, carnival caravans, and strange creatures of the sea; all were painted in fluorescent colors and strung up in lights and torches. These floats stood over a story high and were pulled down the street behind trucks or Jeeps. Turquoise, cobalt blue, green, gold, and red satin jackets and knickers bedecked with sequins, glitter, feathers, and golden braids decorated the bodies of the masked men riding the floats. The opaque and expressionless masks hid the identity of the krewe members who looked almost ominous beneath glittering top hats or derbies. These anonymous masked men were the upper-class citizens of the town: the wealthy doctors, lawyers, bankers, and businessmen all decked out in their royal colors and costumes of Mardi Gras, tossing trinkets and plastic beads to the groveling peasants below. As they approached the viewing platforms where their friends and family had gathered, the bombardment began. All manner of "throws" were hurled into the stands: beads, T-shirts, candy, plastic footballs, gold coins, Moon Pies, and plastic cups carrying the emblem of the secret society.

She shivered, not from the cool evening air, but from the strange and frenzied sight before her. He removed his tuxedo jacket and placed it over her shoulders and put his arm around her trying to warm her.

The parade ended at the Mobile Coliseum. There the krewe members joined their families and invited friends to the ball held inside. The King, Queen, and Royal Court of Mardi Gras were introduced in call-outs to the waiting and assembled guests. As the royal members of the court were escorted around the perimeter of the ballroom, guests tossed plastic gold doubloons onto their elaborate trains that dragged behind as they walked. Music from the band swelled as the court led the first dance of the evening. From there the guests joined the dance floor. Bands played and food and alcohol flowed through the night.

A local headline band played in the main arena where they spent most of the evening dancing and trying to be heard above the music. He made sure to dance each slow dance with her, wrapping her in his arms and swaying to the music while his lips savored the softness of her bare shoulder and neck.

Classes resumed after Mardi Gras and once again brought disappointment at semester's end. Her parents now insisted that she apply to another university somewhere that offered more choices and majors than the community college, maybe one she could find an interest in. Separation from the young man would allow her to put all her attention on her studies and future career. She knew that they were right. She had not found a major that interested her at home, as the small college offered a limited selection of courses. It was time to act, and the application was sent off. In March, the University of Alabama accepted her, although on academic probation. Her grades must reflect a B average in order to study there beyond one probationary semester. She was accepted for the fall, beginning in late August, and so she had this one last semester at home. While the thought of starting anew in a true college town excited her, she also worried about him. What would he do when she left? Could she live without him? She was deeply torn—not wanting to envision her life without him, if even for a while. Certainly she would come home and see him, he could visit her, but the thought of being separated from him for weeks at a time scared her. So used to having him deeply involved in every aspect of her life, she could not bear to think of him not being there. Her every waking thought included him, how could she make it if he were not there?

The coming separation weighed heavily on their summer together. He was working full time at a local chemical company in facilities maintenance, while still taking summer classes. He had moved full time to the bay cottage because of its close proximity to his new job. He spent weekends making repairs and renovations on the cottage as he had free time. He managed to take the blue boat out only on occasion. Visits to their beach were rare. She would drive down to visit on evenings during the workweek, and they would try to make some dates on the weekends to movies or concerts. Mostly the time together was spent in each other's arms on the bed in the cottage. More and more he begged her to let him make love to her. As much as she wanted him to, those words and lectures she had heard all her life haunted her and prevented her from giving in at the last moment. Frustrated, he would begin to pull away from her, not wanting to be rebuffed but still hopeful that she would say yes. Slight hints of strain entered the relationship as a result. They found little irritants with each other and were too quick to point them out. Feelings were more easily hurt and habits that were once endearing became annoying.

One evening in early July, she arrived at the cottage as he was just stepping out of the shower. He met her wrapped only in a bath towel. He smelled of soap and his moist skin glistened, accenting his muscular chest, which was tanned and toned. His pleasure to see her showed through the bath towel. No words were said as he immediately took her to the bedroom and slowly undressed her. She thrilled to his touch and was amazed at the loving skill in his movements. As she ran her hands over his body in return, she marveled at his hardness and the power in his hunger for her.

"Anna, please let me show you how much I love you," he begged.

Anna, in complete rapture, found herself giving in. "Yes," she whispered in his ear.

His blue eyes reflected such love for her, she nearly cried.

He took his time pleasing her before he slowly began to enter her.

A loud pounding came from the back door of the cottage. They heard the back door open and slam shut. Anna was terrified. He froze.

"Wait here, do not move," he said, pulling on a pair of shorts and slowly leaving the bedroom.

Anna could hear voices, muffled as she reached for the covers to hide herself, her heart pounding with fear.

He came back into the bedroom, swearing out loud.

"It's my cousins, apparently they have made keys to the cottage as well," he said, the anger in his voice apparent. "They want to go fishing, word is the conditions are favorable for a Jubilee," he added, sitting on the bed.

He leaned over to push her hair back from her face, the moment lost forever. Once again, the pounding occurred as his cousins banged on the outside of the cottage. The breeze blew through the open windows.

"Did they see anything?" Anna asked fearfully.

"I don't know and I don't care," the frustration more apparent in his voice. "I am sorry." He climbed back in bed with her and pulled her to him.

Shouts of Jubilee carried up from the beach. Filled with disappointment, they looked at each other and sighed. Anna reached for her clothes. Deep inside she wondered if anyone saw them. What was truly a lovely moment shattered and soon was replaced with the guilt that Anna allowed to creep into her mind.

They dressed and joined the others outside and indeed the Jubilee was in full-force. Neighbors also made their way down to the beach. He grabbed a net and a cooler, then headed down to the beach. Anna followed behind. Flounder, crabs, and steel gray eels were clamoring at the shore as far as the eye could see. The air was heavy and still, the breeze gone. He and his cousins scooped up the fish and crabs with nets and filled their coolers with the harvest. Word quickly spread up the shoreline as more families lined the beach to harvest the reward from nature.

Later in the evening, as he cleaned the fish at the end of the dock, he described to her the phenomenon that was a Jubilee. Unique to Mobile Bay, he started, when conditions are right, fish are forced to the surface due to lack of oxygen in the water. Some believe that Jubilees are brought on by lack of rain, current flow, or stagnant weather conditions. Others argue that the rising tides and the pull of the moon affect the amount of salt water pulled into the bay. He told her that most Jubilees occur on the Eastern Shore early in the morning. But here on the Western Shore growing up, he remembered them toward the end of summer and after dusk.

She lay back on the dock watching the stars breaking through the clouds, listening as he cleaned flounder. He tossed the filets into a waiting cooler and the fish heads and bones into the bay. She was silent as his cousins joined them on the dock.

Bored with the festivities of cleaning and filleting fish, she drove home around ten o'clock. What she had almost done was what she wanted so badly, to be close to him and share her first experience with him. Over and over she told herself that nothing was wrong with her deep feelings for him. Still, all the lectures on chastity nagged at her soul.

Confused and unable to understand why she was so scared, she put more space between their visits. Her trips to the cottage became less frequent and while there, she did her best not to get back to that guilty place despite his persuasive moves to the contrary. She never told him how scared by the intruders she had been that night and how the guilt ruled her mind.

As the weeks dwindled to days before she was to leave for Tuscaloosa and her new school, her parents demanded that she leave him with the understanding they were to date other people. It was important for her to enter a new college with an open mind and not be tied down in a relationship, they preached. She needed to open her life to the new experiences awaiting her and this included breaking up with him for now. If he truly loved her, they told her, he would certainly agree that this was the best for her. He should date others as well.

She purposely avoided going to the cottage right before she left for college. At the same time, she had put off packing, still in doubt whether she would follow through. But the day to leave swiftly approached. Overwhelmed by the pressure from her parents and fear of her deep feelings for him, she took inventory. She was only twenty years old and not ready for a commitment. She had no meaningful job and no skills, and she had to finish school. She was scared of taking the next step in the relationship, the line she had almost crossed. What she could not do was explain this to him. And as she tried on the night before she left, she knew he was the one who truly loved her.

"My parents are insisting that I date others at school, and you should too," she told him, trying to hide her tears.

"I am supposed to share you and be happy about it?" he asked with anger in his voice. "God, Anna, how do you expect me to react? Me down here, you in Tuscaloosa dating other guys, seriously, I am supposed to think this is good for us?"

"I think it's the best thing for now," she lied.

"Well, then you go and be free, do whatever you want, but don't expect me to be happy about this! Anna, you are making a huge mistake, how can you walk away from all we have?" he said, the color leaving his face and tears welling in his eyes.

"I have to," her voice trailing off and tears flowing down her cheeks.

"Then, what I say or how I feel doesn't matter to you, as your mind has already been made up for you," he whispered in her ear, kissed her cheek, and walked away like the man he was, giving her the freedom she was asking for.

"But, it does matter, because I still love you," Anna said under her breath, but he was already in his car and her words went unheard.

The next day she left for Tuscaloosa, her eyes still swollen from crying herself to sleep. Carolyn, her former co-worker and new roommate, drove as Anna described her last night with him.

"I broke his heart, and mine too," Anna said.

"It will work out if it is meant to be," Carolyn said as she drove. "Aren't you excited? I wonder what our dorm room will look like."

Anna was excited and reluctant at the same time. Looking forward to different experiences and independence, she told herself it was time to grow up and step outside the comfort of her cocoon and attempt to fly. Still, as she began this chapter of her life, she told herself that they would find each other again one day, believing in her heart that he would wait for her.

Chapter Six

Tuscaloosa, Alabama

A COLLEGE TOWN OF 17,000 STUDENTS, Tuscaloosa was steeped in Southern tradition. Classic red brick buildings with heavy white pillars and columns surrounded the green space of the Quad and of Denny Chimes, which sang out the hours of the day and night. Her classes were centered in these buildings. Sorority Row was a short walk across University Boulevard. The Southern mansions bearing Greek letters sat in a majestic row and the football stadium loomed across the street. Her dormitory was just behind these sorority houses. It was one of the older housing facilities centered in the heart of the campus. It had larger rooms and private bathrooms, and therefore reserved for upper-level students. As a junior, she was eligible to live there.

Anna was so lonely the first few weeks that she called home and pleaded to come back. *No,* her parents responded.

The semester had been paid for and she must give it an honest try, one last attempt. Missing him deeply, she called his phone and listened as it rang. Although her many phone calls went unanswered, she still called—because in a small way, it made her feel closer to him. Later, she would learn that the phone had been disconnected, to cut expenses.

Carolyn, Anna's roommate, had transferred with her from the same community college. Having attended high school in Mobile, Carolyn had a large group of friends waiting to welcome her to sorority life. She talked Anna into going out for sorority rush and together they joined a sorority, a necessity if you wanted any kind of social life at the university. Perky girls from all over the Southeast who became instant sisters were dressed in preppy clothes and penny loafers and bedecked in gold jewelry. Many had new automobiles, graduation gifts from wealthy parents, and so they were always able to find a ride to the many fraternity parties, to house swaps to listen to bands, or to visit the local bars and sandwich shops.

Many of the girls were here to find a husband of means, from old money and a Southern family name, to secure a place in society in such towns as Birmingham, Mobile, Montgomery, Atlanta, and Nashville. College filled the time among the inevitable debutante balls or places of royalty on the Mardi Gras court and of course, future roles in Junior Leagues across the South.

A fraternity boy's status was determined by which fraternity he pledged. As fathers and grandfathers before had pledged, so did they, securing a place in the legacy of the house that bore the same Greek letters they were raised to honor. These were the sons of doctors, lawyers, senators, and federal judges who cruised around campus in new Nissans, Oldsmobiles, Audis, and the occasional hand-me-down Mercedes. The football dates of these boys were guaranteed dinner at one of the finer restaurants in town, all charged to their fathers' American Express cards. Rarely had they held a job beyond running errands for the family law firm or working on the country club golf tournament.

Anna chose a major within the School of Arts and Science: fashion design and merchandising. Finding relief that the most of her credits were transferred, prerequisites completed, she was able to dive into classes that she understood and challenged her creativity. She worked with fabrics and sketching dress designs, all the doodles of the last few years now encouraged and graded. Her confidence grew, her grades improved. She had her sewing machine shipped up from home so she could work on her projects in the dorm and not just in lab classes. She grew more and more involved in the sorority social scene, trying to fit into her new town, but still her thoughts turned to her working boy back home. She missed him. Carried hidden in her heart, the love still burned, hidden as an ember.

With her new friends at her side, she explored her way through Tuscaloosa. They visited the local bars to hear college bands sing covers of 1960 and 1970s radio tunes as the sounds of alternative music and punk rock slowly started to creep into bands' sets, record players, and radios of this college town. Such new songs were heard from the bars to the swap parties at the campus fraternity houses as the disco beat faded and the beer flowed. In darkened corners, pot, speed, cocaine, and Quaaludes were offered. With the decade's end came the winds of change, which blew the sweet, musky smell of marijuana through most house parties.

Football season was the key to college life here and one's social life depended on it. No respectable sorority girl would go to a game without a date. It was not done. Hours were spent getting ready for football games, and the sorority houses would empty of girls dressed in their finest dresses, skirts or jumpers, and gold add-a-bead necklaces. All with long hair pulled in ponytails or headbands looking alike down to the Pappagallo shoes. The lucky ones would be invited to their dates' fraternity houses for the pre-game brunch to mingle with the wealthy alumni who religiously returned for home games. Drinking usually began at these functions.

Fraternity pledges arrived hours before the games to save rows of stadium seats for their brothers and their dates. The boys, also dressed as tradition dictated in navy blazers, oxford cloth button-down shirts, ties, and starched khaki pants, hid flasks full of bourbon in their suit coat pockets. The stadium, silent during the week, was frenzied and alive on all those sunny fall afternoons. Bands battled as students, alumni, media, and fans of the opposing teams came to witness greatness. Coaches named Dooley, Parseghian, Devine, and

Bowden dared lead their boys into battle against the legend in a houndstooth hat. A giant called Bear entered the stadium surrounded by Alabama State Troopers, as a reverent hush fell over the Alabama fans.

While she was engrossed in the fantasy of college life, parties, and creating new designs, a storm was raging at home. On September 12, 1979, Hurricane Frederic raced up the center of Mobile Bay, ravaging all in its wake. As the newscaster signed off the evening news that night, he wished the good citizens of Mobile "Godspeed." Frederic arrived in the dark of the night, changing the face of the town forever. Homes were destroyed, roofs were missing, and a steeple lay on the lawn in front of a church it had once crowned. Downtown buildings on the Mobile River were flooded; the historic district and City Hall became unrecognizable.

Hundred-year-old oak trees that lined both sides of Dauphin Street and Spring Hill Avenue lay tossed like toys in the middle of the roads they once graced. Spanish moss that had once hung from their branches disappeared as if it had never been a part of these picturesque streets, and did not return for years. Power outrages were widespread, and teams of workers from out of state worked overtime for weeks before service was fully restored.

Her parents took some damage, yet they were thankful after seeing what neighbors endured. They begged her to stay up at school. They had enough to worry about taking care of themselves with no electricity or running water. She was safer at school. No, she could not bring them any ice. The grocery store down the street was expecting a truck daily and they would line the parking lot waiting to get their share.

Early in the afternoon, the remains of the storm reached Tuscaloosa. The fury that remained in the storm was startling. Classes were canceled, trees were down, and students were encouraged to stay inside their dormitories or places of residence. Frantically, Anna called the bay cottage to hear the empty ring at the other end, or a recording that stated, "All circuits are busy, please try back later." She hoped and prayed that he had gone to his parents' home in Mobile, away from the water and storm surge; surely he had not stayed in the wooden cottage. Yes, he loved the cottage and would have fought nature to protect it, but she hoped he had listened to reason and protected himself farther inland. She paced, cried, and prayed. As hours melted away with busy circuits and failed attempts to reach or hear any news of him, she was able to reach her parents for updates sporadically, but this only added to her deep concern. Her parents had not heard anything from him but assured her that he was sensible and would have sought shelter. So, while fellow students headed to Mobile to survey their families' damage for themselves, she remained at school still listening to an unanswered phone ring four hours away.

Chapter Seven

For What?

IT WAS HOMECOMING WEEKEND, late October 1979, and a sorority sister had arranged a blind date for her, a fraternity boy from "new row." New fraternity row, not quite as prestigious as "old row," was located on the east side of the campus and housed several fraternity chapters. It was newer to the campus and therefore not as steeped in tradition as the more established fraternities of old row.

Southern and Midwestern boys from families that weren't quite as wealthy pledged these fraternities. Her date was a tall, blonde-haired boy from Ohio or Illinois or somewhere in the Midwest. He had an interchangeable name, Steven Davis or Davis Steven, which Anna had trouble remembering at first. Everyone called him Davis so she did too, not knowing if it was his first or last name. He was attractive, and although he had been a swimmer in high school, he did not make the university's team. The competition was too great. Together, she and Davis, along with her sorority sister and her date, set out for the football game and party later that night at his fraternity house.

At kick-off time, the afternoon sun and crystal blue sky were the perfect backdrop for the thousands of red and white pompom shakers in the hands of the multitude of fans. An ocean of crimson and white rose and fell as the game progressed and the fans urged their team on. Virginia Tech was in Tide Country and the fans were wild. In the stands, the fraternity boys and their dates, dressed in their finest clothes, drank bourbon and colas in large white plastic stadium cups. Bourbon from the pocket flasks flowed freely, and as the ice melted, the drinks became diluted and warm. Adding more bourbon to the watered-down beverage improved the taste. By the time victory was at hand, the once handsomely dressed students were sloppy drunk and disheveled, some to the point of falling down. Still more celebrations lay ahead as many fraternities hosted parties after the game, complete with rock music, bands, disc jockeys, and more alcohol. This was homecoming weekend and the celebrations would continue into the early dawn.

After the game, Anna returned to her dorm room and changed into jeans, an oxford cloth shirt, and tied a sweater around her waist. The evening had turned cooler as late October ushered in an evening chill. Davis picked her up at the dorm with a cold beer in hand, and before heading to his frat house, they stopped at a sandwich shop for dinner.

When they arrived at the house, all the furniture had been cleared out of the downstairs in order to create a party room. Already the floor was wet from spilled beer and hooch punch. The music from the band blared far too loud to hear anyone within standing distance. Voices were hoarse from shouting above the music, trying to be understood.

Her date disappeared more often than he was attentive. He danced with girls she did not know. Still new to the school, she searched for anyone she recognized, but mostly stood at the back wall watching the antics unfold before her. The room smelled of sour beer, cigarettes, and sweat. This did not prevent the frat boys from falling onto the wet floor to dance the gator to the wild rhythmic whoops of their brothers. Her date drank beer and smoked too many cigarettes as he joined in the display before her. She did not like beer and tried to sip the hooch punch he gave her, which was so strong it burned her throat as she swallowed it. She looked for somewhere to leave the drink and sank further into the background of the room, wondering how she could escape. This was not fun; she knew no one and wanted nothing more than to be back in the glassed-in room on the bay. She wanted to go home, home to him.

After eleven, the band stopped for its second break. Davis appeared telling her he wanted to get a record album to play while the crowd waited for the band to return for its last set. He grabbed her hand and together they ran upstairs in search of the missing album. Once in his room, he did not turn on the light but pulled her close and kissed her so forcefully it hurt. She pushed away and he laughed. Then, as if becoming angry, he grabbed her again. She pushed away again, feeling the wall for the door. This only encouraged him to push her down onto the unmade twin bed, which smelled of body odor and lack of washing. He grabbed her and roughly fondled her breasts until they hurt, ignoring her shouts to get off her. He continued to push himself on top of her. She could feel him hardening and becoming more aroused by her pleas to stop. He reeked of beer and cigarettes. She turned her head as far away from him as she could, but he continued his bruising kisses as she attempted to struggle. He tore open her blouse and began removing her jeans. Anna was powerless to his athletic strength and he pinned her so tightly that further fighting was useless. He pushed his knee between her legs to spread them and tugged on her panties. So that was it, she thought as tears filled her eyes and the pain riveted her body through to her soul. With a grunt, he climbed off her to light a cigarette and turned on the bedside lamp, and then he noticed the blood on her legs. He pulled on his boxer shorts, sat in the chair by the bed, reached over to the bookshelf, and removed a book. Lying there stunned, she didn't know what to do. Feeling the desperate need to flee the room, she reached for her clothes. He nonchalantly thumbed through the pages until he found the section of the book he wanted. As she dressed hurriedly, he started to read out loud a chapter called "Deflowering" from a popular sex manual, all the while taking drags from his cigarette.

Realizing that her blouse was completely torn, she pulled her sweater over her head even though the room was sickly hot. She fought with all her will to hold back her tears. She was shaking so hard it was difficult to button and zip her jeans. As quickly as she dressed, she fled the room to search for her friend while her date continued to read aloud from his manual. She could not recognize anyone in the party room downstairs, which whirled around her. Her vision was blurred by the tears that filled her eyes. She ran outside for a breath of cool night air. Instead of wondering how to get back to her dorm room, she set out walking. Guided by the light from the moon and with nothing left to be afraid of, she made her way alone across campus. As the music from the parties behind her faded, she could no longer hold her emotions back and she wept out loud.

The dorm room shower could not wash away the smell of beer and cigarettes. The water ran hot on her skin as she leaned against the shower stall and cried. The water mixed with her tears and fell down the drain along with her lost innocence. She had known true love and had decided to deny them both their hunger for each other. Three months ago, she ended the relationship and broke his heart because she was scared—and for what...for this? Could she ever explain to him what was now lost? Would she ever have the chance? She had walked away from his loving arms and his attempts to make love, and the reality of what the act would have been, true love. As she lay in bed that night, she dialed the cottage number. But instead of listening to the phone ring unanswered, the operator announced, "This number has been disconnected and is no longer in service."

Chapter Eight

Lies

"ANNA, THE PHONE'S FOR YOU," her mother called from the kitchen where she was baking Christmas cookies.

"I will pick it up in my room," Anna yelled from the family room.

"Hi, Anna, it's me," he said.

Anna froze; she knew his voice immediately, his sweet Southern drawl, and the loving inflection in his voice.

Anna heard her mother breathing on the other extension.

"Mom, you can hang up, I have the phone," Anna called out to her mother.

"How long have you been home?" he asked.

"I got home a few days ago," she said.

"How are you, Anna," he asked. "Are you happy at school?"

"I am good," she lied, shaken to her soul and trying not to cry.

"Anna, I would love to see you," he began. "Can I come get you and see you?"

Anna was silent and did not know what to say. She had not expected this and was slow to answer.

"Are you okay?" he asked.

"No, not really," she said softly.

"Can I come see you?" he pleaded.

"No, not now, I am sorry. I have to go," she said, hanging up the phone.

A few minutes later the phone rang again. Anna picked up the phone.

"Anna, please," he begged.

"So much has changed," she said, trying not to cry.

"I know, Anna, but maybe we can work through it," he encouraged.

"But, see, that's just it, I can't work through it," she was crying now.

"Anna, what is wrong?" the concern was deep in his voice.

"I can't tell you," she said.

"But you can tell me anything," he said.

"No," she paused, "not this, not now."

"Anna," he said.

"I have to go, just know that I am so sorry, so very sorry but I can't," she trailed off.

"All right, Anna, have a Merry Christmas," he said and hung up.

Anna's mother appeared at her door.

"Was that him? Did he make you cry?" she asked.

"No, mom, he did not make me cry," Anna answered, irritated by her mother's question, sensing that she was worried Anna might go back to him.

"Then why are you crying?" her mother said with concern in her voice.

"Just because," Anna said. "I don't want to talk about it."

She fell face down on her pillows and cried. She just couldn't face him and tell him the lamentable secret she carried. She believed she had failed him and betrayed the love she had for him. All the lectures of her youth foretold of the ruined reputations, she was sullied, tainted, scared, and confused. If she told him, would he feel the same way about her? Would he reject her as damaged and no longer find her desirable? For years, she had heard no less, so she did not disclose her secret to anyone, unsure of what the reaction to her would be. She isolated herself. Withdrawing further by ignoring how badly she had hurt him and herself by ending their relationship. Her only relief, along with a fleeting smile, had come with her monthly period, quelling the fear that she may have become pregnant.

While she struggled to block the rape from her memory, it became abundantly clear to her that she must deal with this alone. Unable to shake the feeling of guilt that she was somehow responsible, she was determined never to mention it to anyone—ever. That way she would be protected from the scorn or rejection that might come as a result.

When the holidays were over, Anna returned to school. He had not called her again and she had fought the urge to call him.

She moved out of her dorm room and into the sorority house where friends surrounded her and filled her need for companionship. There was always someone to talk with and less time to get lost in her thoughts. Anna focused anew on her studies and her grades reflected it. She was determined to finish her classes and earn her degree as quickly as possible. She lost interest in social pursuits and dating; these seemed trivial.

Spring brought new life to campus. On the Quad, the bare limbs of trees filled with new buds and blossoms while the grass was turning green. Students spread blankets and studied on the lawn between the library and Denny Chimes. Others tossed footballs and frisbies while soaking up the sun. At the semester's end, her grades were very high and her parents were relieved and silent in their opinion that changing schools had been the right move for their daughter.

That summer, Anna returned to work in the dress shop where she had worked a few years earlier. Co-workers told her that her former boyfriend had been in the shop asking if she was working there for the summer. Yes, they had told him, but not on that particular night.

Anna was not surprised one evening to look up and see him enter the store. He walked up to her and smiled the smile that lit up his blue eyes.

"Anna, you look great," he said, taking hold of her arm.

The tingling sensation still raced through her body and she could feel her face flush with color.

"It's so good to see you," Anna said, while her voice shook. "What are you doing this summer?"

"I am still working part time at the factory, but most of my free time is spent working on the cottage. I'm repairing it and trying to make it more livable. I just finished installing an all new bathroom. You remember, it desperately needed it," he said laughing.

"Here, look at these pictures I took," he beamed as he showed her.

"Wow, this is beautiful," Anna said as flipped through the photos. "I would love to see it one day."

He looked at her, surprised. "Would you?"

"Yes, one day when we are not working," Anna replied, looking at him as he backed away from her.

"Maybe, I mean, I guess so. Hey, it was great to see you, Anna. I am heading to a movie and it starts in five minutes." As he turned to leave the store, he waved to Anna without looking back.

Anna froze, not knowing if she had said something wrong since he left so abruptly.

He made no further attempt to see her again that summer, nor did she.

Chapter Nine

A Fresh Start

AN EIGHTEEN-WHEEL TRUCK SWERVED in front of her car to avoid hitting a large piece of tire debris left in the middle of the interstate. Startled from her thoughts and memories, Anna hit the brakes to avoid the broken tire. Seeing an exit sign ahead, she pulled off the interstate on the northern outskirts of Montgomery. After refueling her car, she went inside the convenience mart and bought a soft drink before continuing on her journey. She thought of her children and how much she missed them already. Knowing they were safe at school and had each other and their dad to depend on, she focused on her mission to escape, if only for a few days.

As she started back on the road, she slipped a new CD into the player and sang along, but as the interstate merged onto I-65 just south of Montgomery, she found herself once again consumed by her past.

Anna remembered her father telling her he had seen her old boyfriend's name in the newspaper as having graduated in December from the College of Engineering. He had also heard that he had gone to work for one of the new chemical companies on Dog River, in the engineering department.

Anna smiled at the news, knowing how he had worked tirelessly and paid for his school. Pleased that he had reached his goal, she wanted to congratulate him and thought about calling him.

She called directory assistance and got his phone number. Anna waited weeks to call him, unsure from their encounter the previous summer. Finally, in mid-January she called him from Tuscaloosa. To her surprise, this time he answered.

"It's Anna," she said as he answered.

"Wow, this is a surprise, what's going on?" he asked.

"I heard you graduated last month and got a job, so I wanted to tell you how happy I am for you," she said, feeling awkward.

"Thanks, I am so relieved to be finished with school."

"How do you like your new job?" Anna asked.

"So far it's going well, a lot different from school, but I am enjoying it and learning so much more than I ever did from a textbook," he laughed.

"That sounds so good. This is my last semester and I finish in May. I am ready to get out into the real world as well," Anna said.

"I have more news," he added. "I put an offer on a house and you won't believe this, it's right next door to my grandparents' cottage."

He went on to describe his search for a home. Dauphin Island Parkway, which ran along the bay frontage, was lined with homes that had sustained damage in Hurricane Frederic last year and many "for sale" signs lined the road. He had always wanted a waterfront home and this is where he focused this search. An elderly neighbor was moving inland, discouraged by the endless repairs and upkeep demanded by the annual parade of tropical storms and hurricanes. The property abutted his family's land and the dream of a future compound was formed. The home was small and needing serious renovation but it had all he wanted—the bay. The view outside the tiny house was spectacular, and when he looked at the derelict home, all he saw was potential. The east-facing property on Mobile Bay provided the ground to plant his roots.

She hung up, knowing he would never leave the waterfront. As they had joked years earlier, it was his home, his one true love.

Anna graduated in May 1981. Degree in hand, she set out to find work and her future. She moved back to Mobile and into her parents' home. The economy was suffering and jobs were in short supply, so she took a few part-time jobs in retail to pay her expenses while she looked for greater opportunities. She continued designing and making her own clothes, which she proudly wore to work. Before long, Anna was creating garments for friends and a small but faithful client list grew. She specialized in evening and cocktail dresses. Soon, many of her new creations were being ordered and worn by local debutantes. Anna's fashions were making appearances at Mobile's best parties and her clients delighted in these unique dresses, knowing that there was no chance someone else at the party would be wearing the same dress.

Anna's designs caught the eye of Andrew Smithfield, head buyer of the retail fashion chain, Smithfield & Sons. The company, founded in Mobile over fifty years earlier by his grandfather, was committed to providing upscale men's and ladies fashions. So successful was the company in providing quality apparel, the chain had grown to fifteen locations across the Southeast.

When Andrew approached Anna about joining his buying team, she was stunned and accepted the position with enthusiasm. The reputation of the store was well known and unless you were family, it was rare to be hired into the management team. But Andrew saw freshness in Anna's approach to design and admired her taste. He had examined her designs and remarked at the quality and attention to detail that defined her work. He lobbied hard to hire her and immediately took her on his staff and included her in all meetings and buying decisions. Not one collection was placed in the stores without Anna's approval.

Well into his sixties, Andrew was determined to mentor Anna as his successor upon his retirement. She accompanied him on buying trips to the Chicago and Atlanta Merchandise

Mart to select the collections for the upcoming seasons. He especially relied on her sense of style, basically turning cocktail and evening wear over to Anna before she turned twenty-five. In her, he saw great potential and drive. She deeply appreciated his mentorship and worked earnestly with him, taking on each new assignment with determination and a willing spirit. Her efforts were rewarded with raises and increased responsibilities.

When she was able to afford it during her first year at Smithfield's, Anna moved out of her parents' home and into an apartment. She enjoyed furnishing her small, new place and reveled in her newfound independence. Fashion magazines covered her coffee table and fabric samples and swatches spread over her sewing table. She still sketched designs, although Anna rarely had time to create anything any longer. Her sewing machine sat idle more than it ran. But she loved her job and looked forward to the challenges each day brought.

Her progression within the company rattled many who saw themselves as the likely successor to Andrew. But he had other plans. He continued to push her into the spotlight and into the community. Anna headed the charity fashion shows and became the new face of Smithfield & Sons. The society pages were rarely without Anna's photo posed beside a well-dressed woman hosting a fundraiser for a local cause. She traveled to shows in the company's many locations, selecting the right combinations of outfits and accessories to artfully drape the bodies of runway models in Baton Rouge, New Orleans, Birmingham, Pensacola, Montgomery, and Biloxi. Smithfield's was the destination for the finest fashions found in the lower South and Anna's talents and influence boosted the sales and profits across the chain.

She was a woman in a traditional man's world, shaking up the good-ole-boy family network, unheard of in the Deep South in the middle 1980s. Unheard of too was her salary. By all accounts, this attractive woman in her late twenties was earning money and bonuses only a man would earn. She bought her own car without the help of her father or a boyfriend or husband. She owned a stock portfolio, had credit cards in her own name, and saved to one day purchase a home of her own. Shocking on all accounts, especially as most Southern belles were walking down the aisle, giving birth to the next generation of high-society sons and daughters, and joining the Junior League. She had no interest in any of that. She was pleased that corporate life thrilled her.

Confidence radiated from her and her beauty attracted many interested men through the years. She dated a few, but they were not priorities in her life. They drifted away once the relationships ended. Sex was a part of some of these relationships, although it meant nothing to her now. She was not moved. She felt nothing. Flickers of the past would enter in, as the disappointment of the liaison was inevitable. No one could kiss her like he did. No one could touch the depths of her soul as his caresses once had. Yet she would dismiss these thoughts as quickly as she would dismiss the inept lovers' attempts to please her. Work was what mattered now; work was what she loved.

They had made several attempts to see each other over the years but were never quite in the right place in their lives to rekindle what had been. He tried to see her while she was involved with another, or the reverse; her attempts occurred during a relationship he was engaged in. If one contacted the other, they always made sure to see each other, if only for dinner or a drink. Months would pass before they saw each other again. Anna was ever careful to protect herself and the feelings she still carried. She loved him; she believed he still loved her, but the pride and the hurt of the past kept them from expressing it.

He invited her once to see his bay-front home, years after he purchased it. The talent of his handiwork shined through the beauty of the restoration. He had transformed the once-derelict house into a showplace. Years of hard work and all of his money, he laughingly told her, had gone into building his dream. He had never wavered from his desire to live on the water. Together they sat and looked out over the bay and recalled fondly the days they spent together. The autumn evening was cold, and she shivered. Instead of moving close to her, he offered her a blanket that she gladly took. Perhaps the heating system was not yet installed or working at the time, she didn't recall. Her memory was clouded.

As Anna's journey continued, she remembered one of the last times she saw him, when she was working at

Smithfield & Sons. He had called to invite her to dinner at his old friend Thomas's new house. Thomas was one of his friends from high school who also attended the community college. Anna remembered him, his unique laugh and his dark, curly and unruly hair. He was married now, working as an accountant and was hosting a cookout to welcome his friends to his new home.

Anna wore a light blue skirt and white linen blouse, she added some turquoise and silver jewelry of the Southwestern style, which was going to be introduced to customers as part of the upcoming summer collection. The early spring air was still cool, so she tied a cardigan around her neck when he picked her up at her apartment.

"You look great, Anna!" he said with a smile as she locked the door to her apartment.

He was wearing tan-colored jeans and a polo shirt in steel blue, which accented his eyes. As always, she was drawn to his blue eyes.

He opened the car door on the passenger side for her, closing the door and walking around to the driver's side.

"I hear you are the new face of fashion across the Southeast," he said as he started the car. "I am really happy for you, Anna."

She smiled and talked about her job as they drove to the house-warming party.

"I think you will know Thomas's wife, Karen. She went to Alabama around the same time you did, her maiden name was Abbot."

Anna thought for a while and shook her head no, adding that perhaps she would recognize her when she saw her.

They arrived at the party where Thomas greeted them.

"Great to see you, Anna, you look great," Thomas said, hugging her tightly. "What's it been, ten years, maybe, since I last saw you?"

He led her through the family room, introducing her to the five or six couples already there. Anna recognized several people from college as well as from some of the community fashion shows she had planned.

"What can I get you to drink?" her former love asked.

"White wine would be nice," Anna responded as Thomas grabbed her arm.

"I want you to meet my wife," he said to her.

They walked up to a group of three ladies who were looking out the French doors leading to the backyard. Karen's back was turned to Anna.

"Hey babe," Thomas said to his wife, "I want you to meet Anna."

Karen spun around and her face froze, her jaw dropped.

Anna did not recall her from her university days and extended her hand in greeting as Thomas turned to speak to another guest.

"What are you doing with him?" Karen asked coldly. "Are you dating him again?"

"We are just friends, Karen, and have been for a long time," Anna responded, with a defensive edge to her voice.

"I thought he was happy with Elizabeth," Karen said half to Anna, half to the woman on her left.

"Aren't they getting serious?" Karen added.

"I heard she was in Georgia for a while, training for her job," the other guest added. "I wonder if she knows he is on a date with you," the guest said, directing her remark to Anna.

Just then, he walked up to Anna and handed her a glass of wine.

"Hi Karen," he said, leaning in to give her a hug.

Karen stood motionless, trying to catch his eyes as if to ask what he was doing with Anna. The other ladies flashed fake smiles as he greeted each of them.

Feeling extremely uncomfortable, Anna walked to look outside over the yard, commenting on how pretty the gardens were.

Anna tried to stay by his side most of the evening, visiting mostly with Thomas and him and laughing about old times in the blue boat and her many unsuccessful attempts to water ski.

During dinner, the conservation turned to Anna's job. The coolness from the ladies in the group warmed up a bit as they listened to Anna's stories of the behind-the-curtain faux pas on her recent trip to Fashion Week in New York. They asked if she had met some of the celebrities, top models, or even the elite designers. Some, yes, she had. However they were not interested in a fashion buyer from a small chain in the Deep South located in towns with names that they couldn't even pronounce.

A game of Trivial Pursuit was the after-dinner activity. Anna helped Thomas in the kitchen, loading the dishwasher as the others set up the game. Anna listened as two guests just outside the kitchen door discussed the relationship between Elizabeth and Anna's date.

"Why in the world would he bring her here?" one guest asked. "He knows we are friends with her."

"I thought they were serious," the other replied. "We all know he had a thing for Anna, but that was years ago, I just don't understand what he is thinking."

"Should we tell Elizabeth?"

The chatter stopped suddenly as Anna tried to listen for more.

"Let's go play, are you any good at Trivial Pursuit, Anna?" Thomas asked, smiling.

"We will find out." Anna laughed.

The game played out as Anna tried to ignore the glares of Elizabeth's friends. Growing more uncomfortable as the game progressed, Anna was pleased when her date announced he needed to leave because he had to get up early.

They thanked their hosts and left the gathering, much to Anna's relief. However, she did not ask him about Elizabeth or who she was. She left that alone. But she sensed that whoever she was, she mattered to him.

As he walked her back to her apartment, she invited him in, thinking maybe she could finally explain to him what had happened years ago, why she created the distance between them. Perhaps she could find her way back into his heart or just apologize. He declined, having early plans the next morning to go fishing with his cousins. Were they the same cousins who had interrupted them on that night so long ago? She wanted to ask him, but she could not summon the words. He hugged her good-bye as one would hug a relative or a dear friend and walked away.

She stood with her back against the closed door, listening to his footsteps descending the stairs away from her apartment.

In June, the wedding invitation arrived. She stared at the cream stationery embossed with his name and, as if pulled into the air above, she looked down on the dizzying letters that cut the air and pierced her heart. He was to be married at the Cathedral Basilica of the Immaculate Conception on Claiborne Street.

That summer, as he walked down the aisle, she bought a house and a dog and threw herself further into her career.

Chapter Ten

Nothing Lasts in Retail

ANDREW SMITHFIELD RETIRED and the head buyer duties fell to Anna. He was confident with this decision and placed all his faith in her ability. She was given the new title of vice president of merchandising. She was a shining star with impeccable taste, an eye for fashion, and a work ethic he shared. He was leaving his grandfather's company in good hands. All the efforts he had taken to secure the company's future were well left to Anna. What he did not see was the storm on the horizon; the end of the regional chains and the coming advance of the conglomerate chain stores. It started with mom-and-pop grocery stores, the Woolworth's and the five-and-dime stores. They began to fall prey to the large discount chains and big-box stores that devoured acres of land and offered huge selections at deeply discounted prices. One by one, local shops closed their doors forever. Powerful chain stores opened cookie-cutter apparel stores in the local malls with fashions one could find at any of the chain locations regardless of where you were in the country. The local flavor was gone.

Smithfield's was able to hold on for a few years and battled many takeover attempts. Until the day papers were served at the corporate offices in Mobile. A New York investor had been secretly purchasing shares in the company and was now a major shareholder. With this new power, he positioned his appointees on the board of directors and began to orchestrate the daily operations of Smithfield's. He began by firing the strongest financial officers and replacing them with his own people. New buyers were brought in from the United Department Store Group, one of the country's largest department store chains. Rumors swirled that Smithfield's was being sold to United. Nerves within the original management team were frazzled, and all manner of backstabbing began.

Anna had been married now for just over a year to John Horton, a regional sales consultant representing systems operations in warehousing and distribution. They had dated for only about six months when he proposed. Anna was happy in her life and job. She was now in her early thirties and a longing grew. She desperately wanted children. John came along at the right time. They married and he moved into her house.

While she was on maternity leave, the dismantling of Smithfield & Sons was raging at full speed. Co-workers who had been jealous of Anna's many promotions set out to destroy her by befriending the new managers and buyers and taking credit for her many successes. She had no way of knowing they were undermining her position for their personal gain. In her absence, she was left unable to defend her work and all of her contributions before the new management team.

When Anna returned to her office from maternity leave, the man who had deemed himself the heir so many years before was sitting at her desk. He had succeeded in his attempts to take over her duties. Fifteen years of devoted work and loyal service had disappeared before her eyes. So with her severance agreement in hand and knife wounds in her back, she moved with her husband and new son to Atlanta. Within a year the once-great company was closed and its stores sold to United. The new management team had gutted the company, lining its pockets with large bonuses, glittering severance packages, and golden parachutes.

Chapter Eleven

Anna's Beach

ANNA CHECKED HER WATCH. It was now 1:30 in the afternoon. She was close to the northern delta of Mobile Bay as the rolling hills of west Georgia and central Alabama were distant memories now. The flat landscape and tall pine trees that stood in measured rows for countless miles on both sides of the interstate, the growing fields for the many paper companies nearby, had already graced Anna's rearview mirror. The last of the family farms, hay barrels, cows, and horses that made up the scenery for the last twenty miles or so would soon give way to the green, lush growth of the delta. She was glad she had stopped at the McDonald's restaurant in Evergreen, Alabama. This was the last stop before crossing over the swampy marshes and rivers that led to the northern delta. From here on, she remembered, the interstate was raised, providing an aerial view of the delta, rivers, and bogs below. Excitement started to take hold. Anna tried to calm herself, knowing she had more than ninety minutes until she reached her destination. But this was the point at which she always felt like she was almost home. Gone from Mobile for more than ten years, her heart had always remained; this was her hometown.

Anna considered taking the Bay Minette exit but instead choose the longer route to Interstate 10, knowing it would take her through Mobile. She wanted to drive by the old Smithfield's office building in downtown Mobile. The road signs now declared the towns of Creola, Citronelle, and Satsuma, exotic and romantic names for towns on the northern edge of Mobile County. Nothing has changed. The businesses, churches, and strip malls on both sides of the road had a familiarity time had not erased. Now, she was nearing the eastbound merge onto Interstate 10, which she would follow through downtown, the Wallace Tunnels, and on to the Foley exit and her southernmost destination.

Once through the town of Loxley, the road leading south became unrecognizable. Gone were the family farms and old-time gas stations and Southern barbeque joints. Hotels and chain restaurants on vast out-parcels surrounded the sprawling outlet mall that had devoured acres of farmland. A new high school sat on the opposite side of the road. Great change had come to Highway 59 since her last visits, however many years ago that may have been. She could not recall.

Congestion and traffic grew the closer she got to the town of Gulf Shores. Water-themed amusement parks, a zoo, and more restaurants and shops beckoned to her to come in and spend money. During the summer months, these businesses must be overrun with tourists, she thought to herself, even as she was surprised by the amount of activity for November she was witnessing in this once-sleepy town. Large condominiums reached to the sky where the highway ended at what used to be the boardwalk leading to a footpath to the Gulf. Bars, restaurants, and hotels were packed closely to each other, all but blocking the view of the sandy beaches and waters of the Gulf of Mexico. These were the same beaches that had once been lined with family cottages, hammocks, and picnic tables. All were gone now.

At the intersection of Highway 59 and Highway 180, Anna had passed a vacation home rental office. Doing a U-turn at the first traffic light, she turned her car around and headed back, pulling into the parking lot. She went inside to see what homes were available to rent. Normally, the minimum stay was one week, she was told by the agent on duty, but this was off-season and there was one home available for a four-day rental. Anna took it. The rental house was on the left facing the Gulf of Mexico, just before reaching the Gulf Shores Yacht Club and Marina on the bay side.

Anna parked under the house, and noticed that it was a duplex. A car was parked under the right side of the home, a silver Lexus SUV with Louisiana plates. "Great," she said to no one. She sought privacy and solitude, not neighbors.

Several trips up the stairs later, her car was unloaded and she began to explore the house. It was small and in the shotgun style. A bar and seating area divided the living room and ran the perimeter of the kitchen. The master bedroom overlooked the Gulf through a large wall of windows and a sliding glass door, which led to a deck. She looked around the space and smiled at the décor. It was a typical beach house, but Anna found it charming, playing to her need for a beach escape. Decorated in sea foam green, pale blues, sandy beiges, and white, it pulled the colors of the beach into the living space. The white wicker bedroom furniture completed the summer-time theme, while paintings of Middle Bay Lighthouse, shrimp boats, dolphins, and scenes of the beach hung on the walls of the house.

She opened the sliding glass door and stepped out on to the deck. On the right, she noticed a latticework divider, which served as a privacy screen dividing the duplex. She didn't see or hear anyone who might be sharing the rental; the other unit was completely quiet.

Anna put away the few groceries she brought with her from home and carried her suitcase into the master bedroom. She left the sliding glass doors open, allowing the fresh sea air to blow through the home, taking out the stale air of a home that had been closed up for a while. She changed into shorts and a long-sleeved T-shirt and set out to walk the beach.

It was late afternoon, but the sun still warmed the sand beneath her bare feet. The breeze picked up the closer she walked to the water's edge. Overhead, seagulls squealed and dove into the waters below, catching small fish in their bills. Anna turned and headed east up to the point where the Gulf of Mexico flowed into Mobile Bay, letting the waves wash over her feet. The still-warm waters of the Gulf splashed around her ankles. Clearing her mind of her thoughts of the trip, Anna pushed her sweet memories and long-forgotten dreams, empty marriage, and questions of her future that had occupied the miles of interstate into the background. To be dealt with later, she told herself. Tonight she would just savor the sights, sounds, and smells of the place she loved and never forgot. Time had changed the look of her beach with ever-encroaching building and growth, but at Fort Morgan State Park, nothing had changed. The Gulf of Mexico was to her left. The sand dunes off to her right were covered by sea oats and grass and provided nesting grounds for the many birds inhabiting the area. The marshy wetlands beyond the dunes covered acres of beachfront leading to the grounds of the old fort. Driftwood, shells, and the occasional debris from careless boaters had washed up on the shore in front of her. Oil rigs and natural gas platforms sat on the horizon now, but for the most part, the beach was just as she remembered it. A blue heron took flight as she approached, while the sandpipers led the way along the shoreline.

The sun began to sink slowly, taking the day's warmth with it before she reached the point, so she decided to save her exploring until tomorrow. On her way back, Anna sat on a large piece of driftwood to watch as the sun completed its descent into the bay. The night chill claimed the air as she gathered her sandals and walked the remaining distance to her house.

A cigarette or a candle glowed from the deck on the other side of her duplex. As she walked past the deck to the stairs at the back of the house, the glow intensified as whoever it was on the deck drew a drag from the cigarette. Or perhaps the wind intensified the candle's glow. Anna could not tell and did not want to appear to be intruding on her neighbor's privacy as she stepped up the stairs on the side of the home. No sound was made or words were spoken. She hurried inside and locked the door behind her. She lit a fire in the small fireplace to warm the room and to remove the dampness of the evening air.

In the kitchen, Anna found a corkscrew to open a bottle of red wine she brought with her from Atlanta. She took a wine glass from the cabinet and poured. She swirled the red wine in the glass and thought of a toast. The fact that she had stepped out on her own and escaped to her beach was reason enough for celebration, so Anna raised the glass in honor of herself. The first sip tasted warm and mellow as she sat on the overstuffed sofa to watch the fire. She turned on the television, briefly searching for something of interest to watch. Finding nothing, she watched the fire instead and tried to keep the memories of years ago from consuming her again. As the wine warmed her body, it also pulled her thoughts of the past and heavy concerns for her future to the front of her mind. Soft tears welled in her eyes as Anna looked at her life and the choices she had made that led her here. She felt sorry for herself, before deciding that tonight was the last time she would allow herself to do so.

Anna did not fall asleep until well after midnight, and even then, she slept fitfully. The mist rose off the waves in her dream and the salty spray of the sea dulled her view of the dark figure off in the distance. She knew in her heart exactly who it was. The waves were a deep and angry gray, contrasting with the white foam that beat and roared against the shore. Seagulls shrieked from above and flew inland as if a storm were approaching. The winds kicked up behind her as she called out to him to wait. She could see him, but he could not hear her calls over the pounding surf. She ran after him, desperately trying to reach him. The harder she ran, the farther away he slipped. Her mist-soaked clothes and hair weighed her down and slowed her pace even as she struggled to run faster. Still, she called out to him, unable to reach him. Why couldn't he see her, hear her, remember her? If only she could reach him and beg him to forgive her, have him take her in his arms as he had years ago. At last, she feels his touch, his kiss. As her tears of joy flow free, his arms wrap around her tightly, and once again he is hers. From the darkness, someone else appears in the dream and pulls him away, just as she settles into his embrace. As he is pulled away from her, she sees him slipping into someone else's arms. She watches in disbelief and drops to her knees as he disappears into the mist with the other, but she cannot make out just who. Yet, she knows it is his wife. The sweat drips down her chest and neck through her hair and the now-soaked nightgown clings to her skin.

Anna awoke in tears. Sitting up in the strange bed, she cursed the recurring dream and accompanying hot flash. Reaching for a tissue, she dried her eyes and forehead. She threw off the bed covers and put on her robe. Sliding the door to the back deck open, she stepped outside as the ocean breeze tingled and chilled her moist skin.

The stars sparkled brightly across the pre-dawn sky. The steady beating of the waves against the shoreline made the only sound she heard. She was angry with herself, angry at the dream that haunted and teased her after all these years. Always she was left with the memory of an apology never delivered and a love unresolved.

As her marriage collapsed, the dream had become more frequent. Anna had not thought of him in years, except in passing as a memory would present itself or some news of him or his family would find its way to her. But as the reality of her life grew more disappointing and the intensity of what she had lost began to surface, he returned to her thoughts and dreams. Yet, the dream showed her over and over again that he would never be hers.

As the darkness turned to dawn, a door closing caught her attention. She heard the sound of footsteps descending the stairs at the back of the duplex. A jogger appeared, heading to the shoreline, and turning west to run up toward the point. He looked to be in his late fifties, tall and athletic in build with graying hair longer than most men his age. It curled around the back of his neck. Anna watched as he disappeared.

After a small breakfast, she pulled shorts and a T-shirt over her bathing suit and packed a tote bag with sunscreen, a towel, and a book. She took an old straw hat off the shelf in the bedroom and stuffed it into the tote along with some bottled water from the refrigerator.

As she set out down the beach, Anna removed her flip-flops and felt the cool sand beneath her feet. Slowly, she put her feet in the water, and smiled as it swirled and massaged through her toes.

As she walked, she noticed as the jogger appeared up ahead, running toward her. His hair was tousled and his skin shimmered with sweat. Anna noticed his well-toned legs and body as his wet shirt clung to him as the breeze blew his hair away from his face. He greeted her with a simple "good morning" and continued his jog back to the duplex. Anna acknowledged him with a nod and a smile.

Within the hour she had rounded the point and reached the beach on Mobile Bay that fronted the entrance to Fort Morgan. Anna spread her beach towel, dropping her tote as she claimed her seat.

The waves of the Gulf battled the waters of the bay, creating a strange and angry current as if the underwater gods were waging a dispute over which body of water would dominate the other, a never-ending argument within the waters deep. The occasional fish jumped into the air to escape an underwater predator. As the waves rolled on shore, pleasure boats and jet skis ran across the bay while two shrimp boats worked the water. But Anna's eyes looked beyond the activity, searching the western shore, off into the distance, knowing he was on the other side, somewhere.

The November sun warmed her body as Anna's thoughts returned to the long car ride, the night before, and the dream of him. She recalled the last time she saw him about five years earlier; Anna was in her mid-forties. She had just arrived from Atlanta for a visit to her parents' home on the western shore of Mobile Bay. Her parents had made the move to the bay from the suburbs about ten years earlier as part of their retirement plan. The property was just over three acres, with wide beach frontage overlooking the bay. Anna had driven down many times with her children and dogs. This time, her husband was unable to make the trip, constraints of his job, he announced at the last minute.

Anna found it remarkable that her parents had purchased a home less than a mile down the beach from his home and the little white cottage they had secretly visited all those years ago.

Walking around to the bay side of the home on her arrival, her legs began to shake. After all these years, he was there. Anna's heart pounded wildly. How long had it been, she asked herself and pushed her hands through her hair, suddenly concerned about how she looked. He was there, helping her father repair the pilings on the old dock after damage left by a recent tropical storm. As she learned later, this was not the first time he had helped her father on projects on their new home. But there he was working alongside her father. His T-shirt and shorts were wet, revealing his still muscular build. A desire she thought had been long forgotten resurfaced.

His hair was mostly gray and shorter but still had the familiar wave and curls. Older now with a few lines and wrinkles, but still so handsome she thought, noticing immediately the brilliant blue of his eyes. Those eyes that had pierced her soul years ago still held that same demanding gaze as if it were that November day they first met. His face lit up as soon as he saw her. He hurried to greet her.

They visited briefly until her mother call from the house, shattering the moment; his wife was on the phone. He must go. He reached for her hand and kissed her cheek before hesitating. He looked deeply into her eyes with that soul-searching look only he had. She felt it immediately. He still had feelings for her too, and in that fleeting moment, she knew in the deepest corner of her heart that he had never forgotten her either. Quickly, he said good-bye and rode away in his pickup truck to return to his wife, just as he always did in her dream of him. The kiss was still warm on her cheek, the look in his eyes burned into her heart.

The sputtering of a motor caught her attention and cleared her mind of the memory of him, bringing her back into the present. Anna realized that the early afternoon was upon her, so she gathered her belongings, shook the sand out of her towel, and started walking back to the rental house.

As she rounded the point, she noticed the jogger from the morning heading toward her with a crab net in one hand and a cooler in the other. She smiled, recalling the fun of catching crabs in the surf and eating the fresh sweet meat later in the evening. As he approached, she stopped him and asked how many crabs he had caught. He showed her four or five blue crabs bubbling within and trying to climb up the sides of his cooler.

"Years ago," he said, "they were so plentiful you could just scoop them out of the water. But so many fishermen these days drop their crab traps close to the shore." He pointed out the many white bobbers marking traps only a few yards from the shoreline.

"It's a little more difficult to put together a proper crab boil," he added with a chuckle. "But that just makes the chase more fun."

She smiled, wished him luck, and headed back to the house for lunch.

Chapter Twelve

A New Acquaintance

A KNOCK SOUNDED, and the gentleman jogger stood outside the back door of her duplex.

"The crabbing was a huge success," he said, smiling, as he motioned for her to come and see. The cooler was under the house next to his car. He pulled the lid off and proudly displayed the large catch of crabs all wiggling and trying to climb over each other to get to freedom.

"What we need is a true Louisiana style crab boil," he declared. There was a slight hint of the unmistakable accent that was Louisiana. "Do you have dinner plans?"

Caught off guard and genuinely amused by his character, she laughed. "I think I do now."

He extended his hand, and introduced himself as Tim McMillan.

She greeted his hand with hers and said only that her name was Anna.

"Glad to meet you, Anna." Tim was off to the store for some Old Bay Seasoning, Tabasco sauce, lemons, onions, new potatoes, and fresh corn on the cob. He said he would search for some Andouille sausage to make the meal complete. Pouring ice over the crabs in the cooler, Tim reached for his keys in his pocket. She waved to him as he pulled out from under the duplex. She climbed the stairs to her side with a smile on her face.

Arriving home from shopping later that afternoon, Tim produced a large steel pot and cooking stand from the back of his SUV. He set the pot up under the house away from the cars and set his groceries next to the stairs. When she heard activity under the house, she went downstairs to join him.

Tim looked up from his work as Anna stepped down the last stair.

"You look lovely," he said with a smile.

She had pulled her blonde hair up off her neck and wisps of curls fell around her face. She had put some make-up on, something she had vowed not to do while away, but something about the dinner invitation made her want to look her best. Although it was autumn, the warmth, sun, and beach made her want to dress the part of a character in a Jimmy Buffett song, so she wore the one floral sundress she had packed in her suitcase.

She knew she looked pretty but tried to hide the aura of sadness around her. Shyness had always been a way she protected herself initially, perhaps he noticed and found her intriguing, she didn't know and tried to appear confident in herself. She looked years younger than her age, as just a few lines of character creased around her eyes as she smiled. She was very fit and still had a youthful figure.

The sun was shining from behind her, allowing her shape to be revealed through the fabric of her dress. The sun warmed her back and shoulders as she stood by the stair landing. Gazing up at her, Tim seemed spellbound, his eyes lingered on her until he abruptly returned to his meal preparation, and began to whistle a tune.

He filled the large pot with water from a garden hose and motioned to her to bring the bowl of lemons, potatoes, and onions he left on the bottom stair. Lighting the propane burner on the pot stand, Tim lifted the huge pot and set it on the stand. They talked while they waited for the water to boil.

"No Andouille sausage to be found in the cities of Fort Morgan or Gulf Shores." He pulled a folding chair out of the storage closet in the carport for her to sit on. "That would be a punishable crime in Louisiana."

Tim checked the pot periodically and once the water was boiling, he added a handful of salt, the Old Bay Seasoning and sliced lemons. Next he dropped the onions and potatoes into the water.

"The potatoes take the longest to cook," he said with a smile as he hulled and cleaned the corncobs before adding them to the pot.

Tim carried the cooler full of crabs and poured off the water and melting ice into the sand beyond the concrete carpool slab. He was tall, just about six feet, Anna guessed. His hair had once been a dark brown or almost black, but now it was mixed in with silver gray. She liked that the way it curled around the collar of his red polo shirt. He wore khaki cargo shorts and she noticed that his legs were toned and tan from all his jogging, she reasoned. She was surprised to find herself noticing. His dark brown eyes sparkled as he talked, and he seemed to enjoy his work.

"What do you do, Anna?" Tim asked as poured the crabs into the boiling pot.

"I am a full-time mom and part-time designer," Anna answered.

"That sounds interesting, what kind of design?" he asked.

"I have a small business designing heirloom children's clothes, smocking dresses, christening dresses, and wedding party apparel. I do a little work in wedding dresses for brides desiring a vintage look. For the most part, it's children's apparel."

"How did you get into that business?" Tim said as he stirred the pot.

"I used to have a design business in Mobile, years ago. Then I was hired by Smithfield & Sons department stores as a buyer and worked there for about fifteen years and was vice president of merchandising when the stores were purchased by a competitor," she replied.

"I remember Smithfield's. Didn't they have a store in Baton Rouge?" Tim asked.

"Yes, we sure did," she smiled. "My new business grew after moving to Atlanta and friends admired the clothes I made for my children. It all evolved from there. I enjoy the creative outlet it gives me."

"I'd love to see some of your work. Do you have a website?" he asked.

"I do, I will show it to you if you would like," she smiled.

"That would be great," he added, stirring the pot once again.

When the food was finished cooking, he strained the contents of the pot into a large plastic bowl and sent her up the stairs ahead of him to hold open the back door as he carried the large steaming bowl into the kitchen. Tim moved a bistro-style table and two chairs from inside his duplex to the beachfront deck. She helped as he spread newspapers over the table and placed a roll of paper towels in the center next to a citronella candle. He asked her to light the candle as he went inside to open a bottle of white wine. After delivering the glasses and wine bottle to the deck table, he ran back into the kitchen and carried out the large bowl of fresh crabs, corn on the cob, and red potatoes, placing them in the center of the table.

Anna took her first few bites of the meal and found the spicy seasoning was just right. It was not too hot as to overpower the sweetness of the fresh crabmeat, but with enough kick to liven up the red potatoes and corn.

Tim hammered the crab bodies with a small wooden mallet and she watched as he made a large pile of crabmeat before eating any of it. She smiled to herself, but this time did not invade her host's plate. Anna ate the crab as she always did, just as it came out of the shell. Juices from the crab and corn ran down her hands and arms and on to the piles of paper towels she used, trying to have some attempt at good manners. As the meal was finished, Tim wrapped the discarded shells and corncobs in the newspaper and dropped them into a waiting trash bag and then carried them out of the house to the garbage cans outside.

When he returned to the kitchen, Anna went inside to join him and to wash the crab juices from her hands. Together they cleaned up the few dishes and put away the remaining leftovers from the meal. He refilled their wine glasses before they walked back out to the deck.

"So what brings you here alone and who are you running to or from?" he looked into her eyes as he asked.

Anna turned her head, stunned at the question.

Tim saw her defensive reaction and added, "You are not wearing a wedding ring, but there is an obvious tan line on your finger, as if you just removed it. I am sorry if that was too personal. I withdraw the question."

Anna turned her head away, as her hand ran across the finger that once wore a ring. His question had struck a nerve within her. She looked out over the deck, toward the sun now setting on the western horizon. She took a seat on the chaise-style chair and deflected the question by asking him what brought him to this desolate beach in early November.

Tim followed her and sat beside her on a reclining patio chair. "We loved this beach and for years came to escape the demands of everyday life and to find ourselves again."

She noticed he was not wearing a wedding band either. Feeling uninhibited by the wine she asked, "We?"

He looked up at her and said, "Yes, we." He hesitated as he looked out over the water as if to gain his thoughts. "For five years I have come here alone in November, to try to be close to her and relive the memory of the years we shared.

"Barbara was my world for twenty-six years, and this was her favorite beach. She loved the solitude and the unspoiled, undisturbed beauty. Every year around our anniversary, if we could get away, we would find our way back here. She loved to walk the beach, gathering shells and catching crabs. She loved the sounds and smells and the fact that the beach had remained mostly undeveloped, just as we found it on our first visit in 1978."

She could tell he was deeply moved, which made her curious, so she asked, "What happened to your wife?"

"I lost her five years ago," he said as he stood up and walked inside the cottage.

Afraid that her question may have been too personal, she stood up as if to follow him. As soon as she did, Tim returned with a gray hooded sweatshirt and placed it over her shoulders. She hadn't noticed the night air was turning cooler. He pulled a wind shirt over his head and they both sat back down. Wrapping herself in the warmth of the sweatshirt, she noticed that it smelled of talc and aftershave.

"She died on July 27, five years ago now." His voice cracked. "There was a car accident," he said before his voice trailed off. "Would you like to walk?" He stood almost immediately and crossed the deck to the sliding glass door on his side of the duplex. As he slid the door open, she followed him to the back of the unit and outside stairs, still wrapped in the warmth of his gray sweatshirt. Together they climbed down the back stairs and Tim headed out toward the beach. Anna stopped first to remove her sandals and left them at the base of the staircase. The cool wind blew from the front of the home and she was thankful to have his sweatshirt. After stopping for a moment to zip it up, she followed Tim down to the shore.

Once they reached the water's edge, she asked him if he had any children. "Yes," he replied, "I have one daughter, Hannah, who lives in Austin, Texas. She married this past summer and moved from Baton Rouge with her new husband to be with him as he attends law school at the University of Texas. It was a beautiful wedding. I was so proud of my daughter, but it was such a bittersweet day for me, giving my baby away and not having her mother there with me to share in her joy."

"What about you, Anna, you said you have children."

"Yes," she said. "I have a son and a daughter, both teenagers now."

"Are you married, then?" His eyes probed hers.

Hesitating at first and looking out over the darkening night sky, she answered, "I don't know anymore. My marriage is over and quite frankly, I am not sure it ever began. But, yes, I am still married and trying to make sense of a crumbling relationship that never flourished. I came here to escape from all that awaits me at home, and decisions that must be made. I suppose I should rephrase that; the decision to end the marriage has already been made, but first it must be finalized through the legal system." She added, "I am in the beginning of the end of my marriage, filing for divorce and trying to make sense of how I lost myself over all these years."

Holding back tears, she added, "I have returned to the place I love, a place that holds a piece of my heart I lost long ago and never found again." Her voice trailed off as she looked out over the water. "I am here for a few days to find my strength, and a bit of courage to fight the battles that wait for me at home."

He looked softly upon her with a smile of encouragement and then took her hand, pulling her arm through the crook of his elbow, holding it fast. He headed west toward the point. She was happy to have someone to lean on and was moved by this simple but tender gesture.

"Tell me about you, Tim. What do you do?"

"I'm a geologist and am currently teaching at Louisiana State University in Baton Rouge. I have taught at LSU off and on throughout my career. For years, I was in the oil exploration business out of Houston but now I prefer teaching, a slower pace and no travel demands. After I lost my wife, I needed to be with my daughter, home all the time, no more late nights and no more off-shore trips." He bent down and picked up a large shell that washed up in front of him and examined it before tossing it back into the Gulf.

He smiled at Anna and took hold of her arm before continuing. "We were all we had left in this world and I made the decision to move heaven and earth to make sure my daughter knew she was safe and loved, and that she could depend on her dad to take care of her. I could never replace her mother, but suddenly I had to assume the role of both her mom and dad. So I returned to my beginnings, once again teaching at LSU as I had so many years ago. In fact, that is where I met my wife. She was a sophomore and I was a graduate assistant and lab teacher for the geology department when she came through my class in the fall of 1977.

"Barbara was the most beautiful girl I have ever seen. She was petite, just five foot three inches tall, but she had the strongest will of anyone I have ever met. Her beauty was spellbinding, with her long black hair and the bluest of eyes. Her skin was delicate and pale. She was south Louisiana personified and a true Cajun, Barbara Kathryn Hebert, pronounced A-bear. I mistakenly called her name HE-BERT on the first day of class to the great amusement of all the students gathered." He was laughing by this time.

Anna laughed out loud too, remembering a similar mispronunciation during a runway show in New Orleans.

"You see, Anna, I was an Ohio State graduate. Born and raised southeast of Cleveland, and this was my first class as a new graduate student and lab assistant. I had only moved to Baton Rouge a few weeks earlier after being accepted into the graduate program. Not much Cajun spoken up in Cleveland, so the French-Creole names and their pronunciation gave me a heck of a time at first," he smiled. "Barbara was from a small town called Galliano in southeast Louisiana and her father owned a large fleet of fishing boats based out of Golden Meadow. He had primarily shrimp boats, but they did some crabbing and oystering as well. He also owned the fish packing company that supplied restaurants and grocery stores with shrimp across the Southeast; from *Houston to Atlanta*, he used to say. *Seafood is the life blood of the Gulf Coast and Louisiana has the best*, she used to quote her dad."

Tim paused to look at Anna to be sure she was still interested. "They were a hard-working family grounded in the heritage of south Louisiana, their fishing business, deep faith, and the Catholic Church. She was the only daughter of four children and she was fiercely independent and learned early how to stand up for what she wanted. Her petite size notwithstanding, she could hold her own against those three brothers who adored their baby sister."

Tim released Anna's arm and they walked to a large piece of driftwood that had washed up on the beach and sat down together. "I apologize for dominating the whole conversation," he said.

"No, no, I am truly interested," she said. "Please tell me more of your story."

"We became inseparable," he continued with a far-away look in his eyes. "I loved her from the first moment I saw her. She was a gifted artist. She created primitive earthenware and pottery, but she had the most unusual flair with color. She was able to fire her pieces in a way that enhanced their hues and tones. When she began exhibiting her work, in shows and fairs throughout the Southeast, she attracted a lot of attention. About fifteen years ago, she opened a shop in Houston and created consignment pieces for clients all over the world, from local collectors to governors, senators, and actors. One of her larger pieces was ordered by a former president to give as a gift to the daughter of a foreign diplomat on the occasion of her marriage. Several pieces from our personal collection are on display in the State Capitol museum as an example of works from Louisiana-born artists.

"Barbara was just nineteen when I met her," Tim continued. "She struggled so in my class and after many tutoring sessions, I was madly in love with her. She was my first and only love. We were inseparable that first year. She moved out of her dormitory and into my off-campus garage apartment. By midsummer 1978, we learned she was pregnant, and she was terrified about how her parents would react because of her strict Catholic upbringing. She was determined to stay with me, to have our baby, and continue school in Baton Rouge, but her family demanded that she come home. After the summer session, she gave into her family's pressure and left school. They didn't like that she had taken up with a young man from Ohio who was not a Catholic and so they had absolutely no interest in meeting me or seeing for themselves how much we loved each other. For two horribly long months, September and October, we were miserable and forced apart, me in Baton Rouge, and she at home in Galliano."

Tim leaned over and reached for a handful of sand, watching it sift through his hands as he continued his story. "The late summer heat was oppressive and her morning sickness was severe. I was not allowed to visit her, but we spoke secretly every day with the help of her oldest brother's wife Abby, who lived in a small cottage on the family property. During the day while her parents were working at the seafood packing plant, Barbara called me collect from the cottage and we planned our getaway.

"In late October, as the shrimp season was winding down, her father and brothers left for a final three-day trip to the deepest waters of the Gulf of Mexico. Barbara and her sister-in-law told the family they were going to Thibodaux to shop for maternity clothes. Barbara had quietly packed her belongings in a few suitcases and hid them under her bed. When the day arrived, she and her sister-in-law loaded up the car trunk and headed up Highway 90 to me. Holding her in my arms again was the happiest I have ever been. And so that very afternoon we were married at the Justice of the Peace in Thibodaux, and standing by our side was her sister-in-law Abby. October 29, 1978, the best day of my life, was our wedding day."

Tim continued, "Abby waved us off with best wishes and promised not to advise the family of our secret marriage until later that evening. By then we planned to be a good distance away and not able to be found. We couldn't wait to spend a few days alone, having been separated for so long. We needed to share our joy with each other, savor the happiness we felt for our marriage, and the thrill and anticipation of the baby. Only then would we return to her family and seek their blessing.

"We made it here to Gulf Shores with no idea where we would stay and no reservations. There used to be an old motel that stood on the waterfront just east of Highway 59; I can't recall the name," Tim said.

"Was it Young's by the Sea?" Anna interrupted, smiling as she remembered the way the waterfront looked thirty years earlier.

"Yes," he laughed, "that was it, and that is where we spent the first few days of our marriage. Three of the most wonderful days of my life were spent exploring the beach and as you remember, back then there was not much here." Tim looked at her, "If you remember Young's by the Sea, then you must have visited this area around the same time."

Anna answered with a hearty laugh, "Things were quite different back then and it is possible that our paths may have crossed here before. I spent many weekends on the beaches of Gulf Shores, but mostly Fort Morgan during the late 1970s. That's when I fell in love with this beach."

"We found this beach quite by accident," Tim continued. "I have always had a wandering spirit and perhaps in another life I was an explorer. Late one afternoon during our first visit, we headed west in the car on Highway 180. I wanted to see now far it would take us and I had heard that the old Civil War fort stood at the mouth of Mobile Bay. We made the twenty-minute trip from our hotel and drove around the grounds, arriving after closing time and too late for a tour of the fort. As we left the grounds, we noticed a road to the right leading to nowhere and dead-ending at the beach. We parked and walked to the shoreline and up to the point. The fort was clearly visible, silently watching out over the bay. The beach was deserted; there was no one to be found, no one to be seen. We loved the isolation and natural beauty this special place offered, the water, the dunes, and the marshland beyond. The beach looked as it must have looked for all of time, God's pure earth, unspoiled by human hands. We spent hours walking and savoring the sounds of the beach, the gulls, and the rhythm of the waves beating against the shore. We were two lovers alone in the world. It was magical."

Anna smiled as he had so perfectly described her feelings and love for this special place. While developments were indeed moving closer with each passing year, there was still a little bit of the beach left unspoiled and natural as she remembered it.

The breeze off the Gulf blew harder now, sending a chill through her and even in the warmth of his sweatshirt, she shivered.

"Are you ready to walk back up to the house?" he asked, noticing her pulling the sweatshirt around her more tightly.

She smiled at him and into his deep brown eyes, which seemed to be staring into her soul. The intensity of his look startled her, and she quickly stood up and started back up the beach.

"Wait for me," he laughed, following her before putting his arm around her and rubbing her arms to take away the chill.

She looked up into his face and smiled as if to tell him she liked his arm around her. She liked the feel of a man taking an interest in her, even this simple gesture of friendship touched her as a drop of water in a pool of years of being ignored, untouched, and unloved. She liked it.

They climbed the stairway up to their respective doors, hers on the left, his on the right. They stood awkwardly for a few moments, not knowing how to proceed with the evening or to admit that in fact it was finished. So, with nothing left to say, but slow to leave each other, they both hesitated before they said good night. Anna unlocked her door and turned to thank him, but she made no motion to enter the doorway.

Tim reached to her, pulling her to him and then wrapping her in his embrace. A feeling of total relaxation and security swept over her as his arms held her close. Not wanting to break the embrace or end the moment, she stayed in his arms. It felt so good to be held. So safe, so comforting, and so damn long since anyone had held her she thought, but still she moved to pull away from his arms.

"Good night and thank you," she said, looking into his dark eyes that questioned her leaving, eyes that wanted and suggested more. "This was a memorable evening." She closed the door to her side of the house, not looking back, afraid of being pulled out into the night and to him, curious about the attraction she felt for him, a stranger of one day. She was married, for now, or at least until the divorce papers could be signed and the ink dried. But did that even matter as she stood in the middle of the living room, still feeling the weight, the warmth, and comfort of his arms around her? How long had it been she wondered, trying to regain her composure, how long since she had felt the embrace of a man and not wanting it to end? Or yet to have heard the words, "I love you"? Years, she thought sadly to herself as she removed the gray sweatshirt, and fought the urge to run and return it to him. Instead, she held it to her face to breathe in the scent of the man, his aftershave clinging softly to the fleece. She walked back to her bedroom and placed his sweatshirt on the corner of her bed before stepping into the bathroom to remove her makeup, clothes, and to dress in her nightgown. As she crawled into bed alone, she found herself listening for sounds, any sound that might come from the room next door. His room mirrored hers, divided by just a wall.

She sat up and reached for his sweatshirt and pulled it around her like a blanket. She needed the warmth it gave her. Finding herself aroused by breathing in the smell of him, she redirected her thoughts and reviewed the evening they shared. With their evening conversation playing softly in her mind, she fell asleep.

Throughout the night as she slept, Anna was fully aware of the oddest dream taking over her mind. Someone was holding her close. It seemed too real to her to be a dream, as she lay there alone in the bed. She was being held in someone's arms from behind, spooning and wrapping his body closely around hers, melting his body into hers. She could feel every contour of him but could not see him. His desire was to hold her closer still, not letting go, wanting her more as she tried to yield to him, her body moving into the imaginary lover, his presence so strong and real in her empty bed. His muscular and protective arms were holding her as if to never let her go. And she knew in her deepest sleep that he loved her, but she did not know who this companion was.

Chapter Thirteen

Searching the Western Shore

DAYLIGHT CAME WITH THE SLAM of the back door and Anna was startled from her bed. Awaking from a restful night's sleep, she felt vibrant and renewed even as the bedside clock read six a.m. Grabbing her robe, she threw back the covers and Tim's sweatshirt fell on the floor. Opening the louvered blinds to the back deck, she watched as her new friend started his morning jog toward the point and the bay ahead. Anna picked up his sweatshirt and held it to her face before placing it on her bed.

She turned on the coffee pot and started the shower, all the while feeling the need to visit the one place that called to her heart. She wondered if it was still there. She had not considered going as she drove yesterday, but something tugged at her now. She wondered if she had the courage to go, what would she find if she did, what would be accomplished? She searched the kitchen drawers for tourist information and found the schedule for the Fort Morgan ferry. The first car ferry left for Dauphin Island at eight-thirty. She had time to make it. Anna ran to the bathroom, showered, and dressed quickly before grabbing her coffee mug, purse, and keys. Locking the cottage, she ran down the stairs to her car parked under the house. For some reason she wanted to be gone before Tim arrived back from his run, fearing she might otherwise change her mind. Knowing she could be easily talked out of going. She started her car and drove the short distance to the loading point near the old Civil War fort.

Only a few cars waited in line for the ferry and Anna was confident she would make the first departure. She noted the return times, since this was November and the fall schedule provided fewer opportunities back to the fort. She wanted to be certain she could return to her rental house via the ferry rather than make the ninety-minute drive back over the bay. As she waited on the loading dock, Anna noticed the name *Alexandria Nicole, Dauphin Island, AL,* in blue letters painted on the bow of the white vessel. A beautiful name she thought. Perhaps named for the captain's daughter. Or for an unrequited love of the captain gone from his life, but not from his memory, Anna romanticized.

Anna looked at her watch. In just five minutes, the ferry would begin loading the passenger cars. Trying to remember that last time she boarded this ferry—years, she thought to herself, maybe ten. She recalled when the ferryboat service began after Hurricane Frederic. The only bridge leading to the island from Mobile was heavily damaged in the hurricane and condemned. Ferryboat service became a necessity as the new bridge was being built, carrying island residents back and forth to Mobile. Upon completion of the new Dauphin Island bridge, ferry service was no longer needed into Mobile. So the wildly popular service from Dauphin Island to Fort Morgan was introduced and remained in place thirty years later. Tourists and locals loved the quicker water route to the beaches of Gulf Shores. During the summer months the waits were hours long for the two ferry boats crossing the thirty-minute stretch of water.

A whistle sounded and the procession of cars moved forward, filling the ferry as the flagman waved them onto the vessel. The gate closed, the motors revved. Anna felt butterflies of anticipation dancing within her.

She got out of her car and stood along the side railing of the ferry, enjoying the sights as the vessel set out across Mobile Bay to Dauphin Island. Pelicans stood on the dock pilings and took flight as the ferry passed. Anna watched as the birds flew above and then marveled as they dove straight into the water to catch their prey. The morning air was cool and clear as the last strains of Indian summer played out over south Alabama. The water sparkled as they rode across the waves. The sunlight warmed her skin. The breeze was too strong for a hat and as the ferry hit an occasional wave, sea spray splashed on the passengers at the rail. Anna enjoyed the breeze on her face and the bouncing and rocking motion as the vessel crossed the bay.

As they approached Billy Goat Hole, the landing place for the ferry on Dauphin Island, the glare bounced off the white sand dunes that buffered the channel. Anna was thankful for her sunglasses. She got back in her car and waited to be waved off the ferry. She followed the line of cars up the road to the island's only traffic signal beneath the water tower. She turned right and headed over the bridge and onto the main land headed north toward the small town of Theodore.

The butterflies of anticipation quickly turned into nerves. Her heart pounded wildly as her hands gripped the steering wheel, she tried to stop trembling. To no resolve, her whole body was shaking now. The closer she got, the more paralyzed she felt.

She did not pay any attention to the miles of scenery along the two-lane road until reaching the four-way stop with two churches on the east corner and a produce stand on the west. Less than half a mile up the road was the driveway to the secret cottage. Unsure if she would recognize it and what she would do if she did, she softened the pressure on the gas pedal, slowing the car until she came to where the old gate still straddled the driveway. She pulled in and stopped. A chain was wrapped several times around the gate and locked with a heavy padlock. For that she was greatly relieved. There was no possible way she could pull any farther up the drive and she felt certain that she did not want to leave her Tahoe parked there to walk up the long driveway toward the secret cottage. However, standing there in front of the gate, sizing it up, she knew she could climb over it. Hesitating for a few minutes, she looked back at her car and around to see if anyone was near. She grabbed the top of the metal gate and pulled herself up and jumped down inside the gate. She started walking quickly so as not to be seen by any passing traffic. The gravel and oyster shells beneath her feet soon turned to blacktop pavement the deeper into the property she walked. She could feel her heart pounding with exhilaration and the dangerous feeling of sneaking somewhere she did not belong. Sweat broke out across her forehead as the sun warmed her skin. She wondered what lie ahead. Tall bushes on both sides of the driveway soon gave way to more manicured hedges, crepe myrtles, and sculptured landscaping. Anna looked up to see a Mexican tile roof rising above the foliage. Her heart sank.

"It's gone," she said gasped.

She reached the driveway's end and before her stood a beautiful new home. Rich in traditional Spanish architecture, the sprawling home covered the spot where the secret cottage once stood. The yellow stucco exterior—dark heavy wooden doors and shutter-framed windows—spoke of a villa. The red-tiled roof complemented the structure graced by lush palm trees and window boxes laden with tropical flowers. Through a rounded archway on the home's façade, the driveway weaved around the house and ended at a three-car garage to the left. A swimming pool and cabana were clearly visible through the archway and a new dock and boathouse reached out onto

Mobile Bay beyond. A tall cypress privacy fence surrounded the property, preventing any view of neighboring homes. His home specifically, just on the southern property line.

The villa appeared deserted, for which Anna was thankful as she was clearly trespassing. She stood and marveled at the beauty of the home while feeling a pang of sadness that the cottage was gone. It was inevitable, bay front property was valuable and thirty years ago the cottage was in need of repairs. He had done what he could, but the cottage could not have survived the years without serious renovation. Memories of what had once been flooded her mind as she turned and walked back to the car. Anna's heart was heavy, the excitement gone. Time moves on, she told herself, nothing stays the same.

Anna reached her Tahoe and pulled herself inside and started the car. She backed out of the driveway and drove to the corner produce stand to settle herself. Anna breathed a huge sigh of sadness as she parked. Why, she wondered, had she set out this morning to see the cottage. What had she hoped to find? Would it have settled any questions if she had seen their secret cottage one more time? What was she doing here, chasing the ghosts of her past?

Slowly she got out of her car and made a few random purchases: a tomato, a cucumber, and red bell pepper. Thanking the clerk, she got back into the car and headed south back toward Dauphin Island. Coming up on the left was the road where her parents had moved over a decade ago during their retirement years. She turned on her left signal and made the turn following the road to its end, a bluff overlooking the bay.

She parked on the road alongside the fence surrounding the old family property. A "For Sale" sign greeted her at the front gate. Anna walked up the brick pathway to the side door. The red birdhouse still stood on its post by the now-empty cement fountain her parents had placed by the side door. The fountain had once bubbled over with white foam after her children had poured in the contents of a plastic bottle of children's bubbles. She looked around her and smiled, remembering all the happy times in that vast yard. So many were the sweet memories here: her young children, nieces, and nephews splashing in blow-up pools and running through sprinklers. The hours spent chasing and spraying each other with water guns to the sounds of giggles and glee. Badminton and volleyball tournaments, and baseball with red plastic bats played out on that front yard overlooking the bay. Always there was the sound of laughter, music, and the smells of food being cooked floating out from the kitchen.

Anna remembered fondly her old German shepherd chasing rabbits, shadows, tennis balls, or anything that moved. If the dog could not find a ball to be tossed, she would bring one of the many large pinecones that littered the yard to drop at her feet to be retrieved instead. That long-deceased dog loved the property as much as Anna had. She could almost see her running across the yard after another pinecone. Surely this was heaven for any dog.

Two years earlier, Anna had helped her parents box their possessions as they prepared for their move to an assisted living center close to her home in Atlanta. The expanse of property had become too much work for her father, as the demands and upkeep of living on the water were better suited for a younger man. Yet for close to a decade, her family had loved this old home and made countless trips here for visits. Oddly, it still felt like home.

Anna rang the doorbell, to no answer. She walked around the front of the house noticing the decline in the quality of the yard care. The once lush gardens where overgrown with weeds and large tree branches were scattered about the yard. Bushes were overgrown, shapeless, and heavy, and the lawn needed mowing. She walked around to the screened in porch, which faced the bay. She pulled on the handle, which immediately yielded to her. Many of the screens were torn and swaying in the breeze or missing altogether. Anna stepped into the porch area and rang the doorbell on the door leading from the porch to the living room. Again, no one answered. Cupping her hands to her eyes and looking inside, she saw the house was empty. She tried the door handle, discovering it was unlocked and opened at her touch. She looked around her to see if anyone was watching, but there was no one in sight. The old home was surrounded by trees and hedges on both sides and by Mobile Bay out front. Anna slipped inside unseen. Silently the lonesome house greeted her, a house once warm, loved, and filled with family now stood deserted, stale, dusty, and unwanted. As she stepped inside, memories came flooding back.

The paneled living room and its magnificent views of the bay had not changed at all. She next walked into the kitchen. The appliances had been stripped from the house, but the cabinets her parents had installed were still in place. The bedroom off the kitchen was the same color blue it had been painted ten years earlier. Anna stepped down on to the brick hallway leading to the long dining room, office, and additional bedrooms in the back of the house. She did not go farther back into the house, stopping at the doorway to the bedroom that had been her parents. Suddenly she felt uneasy. She had never witnessed it herself, but family members had been sure this room was haunted. They had talked of the voice of a young man calling out for his father deep into the late hours of the night and an accompanying dark silhouette that shrouded the doorway. Memories of her father sharing his encounters with the odd voice over the years sent a shiver through her and she hurried back to the front of the quiet and empty house. Feeling uncomfortable for trespassing, she returned outside to the screened porch and pulled the door closed behind her.

She walked out across the unkempt front lawn toward the bay and stopped at the seawall edge looking out at the water. A neighbor's dock was completely gone now and the only evidence that one had existed were pilings standing in varied positions of attention, jutting out of the water holding nothing. The sandy beach below the seawall was in disarray, evidence of a busy season of tropical storms. The storms had played havoc with the abandoned property, with no one to clean up after. Driftwood covered the beach, and the stairs her father had built leading from the dock to the beach were gone, washed out to sea. The long dock was still in fairly good condition, weathered and gray with some boards missing. It was crooked, as many pilings had shifted in the waters causing the boards to sway and buckle, but still it was passable, so Anna carefully stepped out onto it. Walking slowly, inspecting every step so as not to fall through a rotten or missing board, she made her way as far down as the old gray dock would allow her to go. The breeze off the water blew Anna's hair wildly; she wished for a barrette or something to hold it off her face, but had left her purse locked in the car.

The bay was quiet, with the exception of one passing barge being pushed by a red tugboat up the shipping canal toward the shipyards in Mobile. Gulls shrieked overhead as the waters lapped about the dock pilings. She looked up the shore, north, trying to see his house, just barely visible as the land curved inward. The white house sat high on the embankment just before the view was obstructed. An American flag flew above his dock, the only activity at his home she could see from her safe distance on the old dock. It was mid-morning. He was likely at work, his children at school. Beyond his home, Anna could just make out a glimpse of the red-tile roofline of the villa. Over the years as she had walked this old dock, she would always find herself searching north, trying to see that old secret cottage, perhaps him, or something of her past.

A stern-looking man calling from the front yard startled her back into reality. Her heart stopped, looking up at him, but she decided to wave back as if she knew him and she belonged there. She took one final look up the bay and turned to walk back to the house, mindful of the damage to the dock.

"What are you doing here?" the man called gruffly to her as she approached the yard. His face was scowled and his brow lined in a deep frown.

She was frightened by his demeanor but quickly decided to be as pleasant as she could, calling back to him, "I saw the for sale sign out front and stopped to pick up an information sheet, but the tube was empty. I am here from out of town looking for waterfront properties. Are you the owner?"

"No," he said as his face softened. "I have the listing as realtor, but this house is by appointment only."

"I had no way of knowing that," she lied and added, "I was intrigued by the view of the bay and felt the realty sign was enough invitation to look around. I am sorry for any inconvenience, I will go now."

She turned from him and started back to her car as he called from behind.

"No, no," he said. Realizing the opportunity for a sale, his attitude and demeanor changed and he added, "I am here and would be happy to show you around. Do you want to see the inside?"

She felt extremely uncomfortable around this man and did not want to enter the house with him. So she said, "No, thank you. It is the property I am interested in; this house is outdated and needs to be torn down. I have no interest in going inside. My architect would be the one I would ask to offer suggestions on how to proceed with rebuilding. Do you have any information with you on the property and lot size or a business card you could leave with me so I can contact you later?"

They walked around to the side of the house where Anna's car was parked and he reached into his jeans pocket and produced his business card advising her how he could be reached. He gave her the asking price of the house and commented on her Georgia license plate. Trying to be pleasant, he encouraged her to call him in about an hour when he would be back in the office and could give her the details she needed on the property. All she wanted to do was leave, so she thanked him saying she would do just that and got in her car, immediately locking the doors as she smiled a fake smile and waved at him. She turned her car around in a neighbor's driveway and pulled away down the street.

Anna hesitated at the intersection, before heading south, back toward Dauphin Island. Disappointed, but not sure why, she reasoned that she would never recapture what was lost. Driving the road map of her youth could not bring those years back to life, no one knew she was there, no one knew she still cared.

On the return trip, she took the time to notice how little the road to the island had changed over the last thirty years. Cottages and houses along the road sat high on pilings and trailer homes sat on cinder blocks to prevent being flooded during hurricane season. Seafood restaurants decorated both sides of the road, mingled with a tiny used car lot, a dollar store, and the foreign legion hall. Bait shops and tacky bars beckoned drivers heading to and from the island. And a once-proud fishing boat, weathered and worn, sat in its honored place up on pilings of cinder blocks on the front yard of a small home where it had been for the last twenty years, never again to conquer the waters on Mobile Bay.

The land narrowed and the bay was clearly visible on her left. Farther south the waters were dark and murky, marshland and bogs to her right. Narrow canals were carved out along the roadside to accommodate the oyster boats secured in the marshy waters just before the base of the high bridge looming ahead. A fishing pier lined with old men hoping to catch the evening meal was her last sight before her car started the climb up the bridge. At the highest point, the most beautiful view of Dauphin Island and the Gulf of Mexico stretched out before her. Tiny sand islands, the landing pads for thousands of birds, chained out from the base of the bridge leading to the channel. Fishing boats, tugboats, and a few pleasure boats ran across the waters below.

At the end of the bridge, a large marina, Ship and Shore Supplies store, and other businesses lined the roadway, beneath the white water tower painted with the greeting *Welcome to Dauphin Island.* Anna pulled into Skinner's Seafood Shop and purchased some fresh shrimp before driving to the ferry launch.

She got in line behind two or three other cars waiting for the 1:30 departure of the ferry. Opening her car windows and sunroof, she enjoyed the salty sea air while she waited. A boater backed his boat and trailer skillfully alongside an adjacent dock and into the launching area where, on any given weekend, there would have been dozens of boaters in line waiting to launch their boats. Today it was quiet. His companion waited on the dock, holding the ropes as the boat released from its trailer.

As the ferry began to load the cars in front of her, she watched the two men venture out at idle speed into the canal leading out to the Gulf. The sea air blew through the open windows and sunroof as Anna followed the flagman's direction, parking on deck. Soon the ferry ride got underway.

Anna reached for her purse and removed her wallet, thumbing through the many photographs of her children. She missed them already. She pulled out a photo of her son and daughter taken the previous summer from the plastic holder encasing it. Out from behind the photo fell another taken years earlier. Then there were only three in her family: her son who was about five years old at the time of the photograph, her husband, and herself. She was wearing a pale blue linen blouse and white pearls. She remembered how she had dressed her son in a white polo shirt with a soft blue embroidered emblem for the portrait. Her husband was wearing a blue oxford cloth button-down dress shirt. They matched, a happy family enshrined in a photo. What she remembered from that day, she still saw there in her eyes.

They had fought that morning. When the photographer said smile, Anna remembered wanting to look happy but she didn't know how to at the time. She vividly remembered telling herself to think of her first love and to try to recall just what it felt like to be happy. Perhaps the memory would glow through her eyes, deceiving the camera. But the resulting photo did not lie. The camera had captured her sadness. She slipped the family portrait back again under the newer photo of her children, and closed her wallet.

Looking out over the water, Anna thought of other photographs taken through the years as the ferry made its way across the bay. Her husband had had pictures scattered around his apartment while they were dating. In them, he was engaged in daring and exciting activities. In one, he was dressed in full rock climbing gear; another showed him positioned with one foot on a windsurfer as if to set sail. An eight-by-ten framed portrait of him standing in front of a scuba shop sign holding a mask and flippers was centered in its place of honor on his fireplace mantel. She had never watched him participate in any of these activities. His scuba gear had been moved from house to house still in its original packaging, never to be opened or immersed in water. As the popularity of rock climbing clubs sprang up with indoor venues opening around Atlanta, she suggested he join and take a class, but the attempt was never made. Why then the photos, she wondered all these years later. Were those activities something he gave up in his marriage? Or were the photos merely his attempt to be adventurous, flirting with danger but never having the fortitude to pursue? Was there a wanderlust or appetite for adventure that she had stifled, or were these dreams he chose not to live out? Whatever his reasons, she felt that she had never known his inner self, the true person that he was. Fantasy engrossed him as a substitute for real life.

She pulled into the driveway, parked under the duplex, and gathered her belongings and the bag of produce from the passenger's seat. She walked around to the back of the Tahoe and opened the tailgate, lifting the small cooler containing her seafood. She carried the items inside and went into her bedroom. She opened the sliding door and walked out onto her deck to look out over the water. The day had grown too warm for blue jeans, so she turned to step back into her room to change clothes.

"I was afraid you had gone without saying good-bye," Tim said from behind the latticework that divided their decks.

"Oh, no, I was visiting an old friend," she lied, startled by the break in silence.

"Would you care to join me on a walk?" Tim asked as she pulled the door closed.

"I will be down in a minute."

Chapter Fourteen

The Unraveling

ANNA PUT ON A PAIR OF ATHLETIC SHORTS and a T-shirt. She pulled her hair into a baseball cap and put on her sandals. Catching her reflection in the bathroom mirror, she looked about thirty years old. Still thin and wearing the same dress size she wore in college allowed her looks to defy her age. Her legs were toned and still shapely and the athletic shorts accentuated this fact. For years she had enjoyed various forms of exercise and found that she needed the freedom it gave her to clear her mind of stress and the difficulties of her home life. She smiled at her reflection and hoped Tim would notice as well.

She locked the back door and hid the key behind a planter on the landing. She had no pockets and didn't want to hold anything in her hands, wishing he might take her arm in his again. Tim was closing the door to his side as greeted her with a brilliant smile. Together they walked down the stairs. She stopped briefly to remove her sandals and left them on the carport slab.

"So where did you go this morning when you left so mysteriously?" Tim asked as they started across the sand. It was obvious that he did not believe she had been visiting an old friend.

"I took the ferry over to Dauphin Island," she started, "in an attempt to see someone who was very dear to me, someone I loved very much, someone I never let go of. Honestly, in my heart, I did not believe I would see him today, but I wanted to walk through the memory of a place we had once shared."

They greeted a fellow beachcomber, and the only other person that she had seen on the beach since her arrival. She looked up at Tim as if for encouragement before continuing.

"As fate would have it, the cottage we shared many years ago is gone, a new home in its place. His home is just next door but I could not bring myself to trespass onto his property and into his life. He is married and has been for years. I just wanted to see him and possibly talk to him. But, it is probably a good thing it did not happen. The message is too deep and personal. You see, I have an apology to deliver that is thirty years overdue."

Anna was thankful for the sunglasses that covered her eyes as they welled with tears. She continued, "My story is somewhat similar to yours, but instead of following my heart, I listened to the words of my parents and allowed us to be separated and ultimately the relationship ended. I left him brokenhearted and alone while I tried to do what was expected of me. I always believed he would come back to me and we would end up together, but the circumstances of my life and decisions I made along the way prevented such a happy ending. And someday I hope to gather the strength to tell him the truth—if the opportunity ever presents itself."

Tears slipped beneath her sunglasses and down the side of her face. Tim reached out and wiped them from her cheek. He laced his arm through hers as they walked up the beach.

"This was our beach, our hidden treasure," Anna continued. "We loved it here just as you did. Any chance to escape here, any weekend during the summer you could find us here. We loved the privacy, the undisturbed beach that stretched for miles, and the fact that not many people were around. We swam, walked the beach in search of crabs, and loved each other on a beach blanket under the bright summer sun.

"Love was pure and simple in those days," she continued. "There was no resentment, no rejection, no constant controlling or belittlement of one's spirit, just pure innocent love, untainted by all the disappointments that seep into life. But, he did not wait for me, because I failed him. He married another and I was the one who lost out and let him slip away forever."

"So this is why you came here this week, to visit someone from your past?" Tim asked.

"No, actually that was not even part of my plan; for some reason this morning when I woke up I had a strong need to go, to flee to the other side of the bay, and why, I do not know. I just knew I had to go."

"Why then did you come here all this way from Georgia?" he questioned. She did not have a direct answer. For strength, for redemption, for the girl who was once strong and now lost, for the memory of the love of her life, to touch her roots, to find renewal and courage, to remember that she was once loved and deserved to be again. She could not share this with him, so she said simply, "To find some peace."

"What of your husband? Does he know where you are?" Tim asked.

"I told him I needed a few days to myself and that I would be home on Saturday but I did not tell him where I was going. He does not know this place. It was not his to share with me. That belonged to someone else," she added, "I did speak with my children before they left for school this morning. Since cell coverage is spotty here at best, I told them I would call when I could get a signal. They know I am fine and that I love them and miss them and that I will be home in a few days."

"Did you ever love him?" Tim asked, trying to study her face.

"My husband? I don't know," Anna paused, looking up at him. She was surprised by his question. "I think I was in love with the idea of being in love. I don't really know what love is anymore. Funny, I question myself about this all the time: do I love him, did I ever, did he ever love me? I just know there has to be more for me than this. So in answer to your question, no, I don't think I ever did.

"I was thirty-four years old when I married and longed desperately for a child," she continued. "I believe now that I let that rule my decision for marriage and found a mate who offered little in the area of love. He was too caught up in the façade and fantasy of himself. I felt like I was living Act Two in the play of his life. Life together was never about growing close to me or creating a strong relationship and stable home. It was always about him and how the world saw him."

He looked at her through questioning eyes, encouraging her to speak freely.

"I knew on my honeymoon that something about the relationship did not feel right. But I pushed those feelings away, blaming myself for having a preconceived notion of what married life would be like. No, I told myself, I was just living in a fantasy left over from my childhood. Life doesn't provide a happily ever after, and all that falls in between can't be unending happiness and wedded bliss. Dinners out or date nights were never even thought of in our marriage. Friends took special vacations, a second honeymoon, or weekends away from their children to focus on one another and dedicate time to each other. We never did. Perhaps once or twice we went out for an anniversary dinner."

She fell quiet as they walked around the point toward the fort. One particular New Year's Eve party, the reality of her life had become stunningly clear. Friends had gathered to celebrate the evening together and the midnight hour was greeted with cheers and confetti, as the couples locked in embraces and kisses. Her husband awkwardly kissed her with the kiss she had grown to hate. A kiss with no passion, no strength, no meaning; over-puckered, pursed, and strangely soft. A kiss to be delivered on a grandmother's cheek or a swift greeting of a relative not liked but merely tolerated. Afterwards, she stood next to him and watched her friends around her still wrapped in their husbands' arms, being kissed with meaning, with love, and with the promise of celebratory lovemaking later that evening. It was as if reality had slapped her cold in the face, she felt so uncomfortable wanting to escape the moment as she stood watching. He too soon noticed the other couples still wrapped in loving embrace and bent to try to deliver another meaningless kiss. She turned away, never wanting another of his kisses.

All the kisses they shared were dispassionate and empty. His feeble attempts at lovemaking were unskilled and hurried. Her requests and suggestions were ignored and he became offended at the implication that he was anything other than wonderful. He was always posing and watching himself with one eye on the mirror. So many times during sex she thought this must be what it is like to film a love scene in a motion picture, as actors merely going through the movements while the room was filled with cameras, directors, make-up artists, and sound checks. And so she was left empty, never touched, and wondering why and how she had come this far away from knowing love.

What had made her settle for this, what made her give up on herself? The rape had changed everything, and more than she cared to recall or relive, it was the damnable rape. She had never faced the reality of or forgiven herself for all it destroyed. She still carried the guilt and the shame and believed that she should have prevented it from happening. Somehow it was her fault. Never dealing with the outcome had forced her to look down on herself all these years and therefore she denied herself any pleasure or closeness. It had been easier to block the memory and ignore the wound. Still, it festered within her, holding her hostage over the years. It seemed only natural that she attracted a mate who lacked the interest or ability to be intimate. It was easier that way she now realized; her secret could remain buried in her soul and no one would ever discover that she was damaged and unworthy of being loved. She had married a self-fulfilling prophecy.

Tim looked at her, expecting her to continue after her long silence, but she did not. Instead she looked out over the water, turning her eyes from him. There was nothing about this memory she cared to share with him or anyone, ever. A distant rumble of thunder caught her attention. It was time to turn around and head back to the rental house.

"I am going into Gulf Shores tonight to meet some friends for dinner. Would you care to join me?" Tim asked.

She paused, thinking. Yes, she would like to spend the evening with this interesting man if he were all hers, but given the choice of sharing him with yet unknown acquaintances she begged off, explaining that she needed to be alone with her thoughts. "No, but thank you. Tonight I think I will just stay in."

"No problem, I understand." He smiled.

The wind off the Gulf picked up as the thunder grew closer and the churning waves turned the same color gray as the heavy storm clouds above. In the distance, rain moved across the Gulf, further dulling the horizon where the water met the sky. The white sand and the foam from the waves gave the only contrast of color as small drops of rain began to sprinkle down on them and the thunder boomed. The wind blew her baseball cap off and her hair tousled wildly in the rain. She bent to retrieve the cap and he took her hand and together they ran back to the duplex.

By the time they reached the duplex, they were both soaked through with rain. They stopped inside the carport to shake off the rain and she gathered her sandals. Waiting for the rain to stop was useless as it continued harder and harder, pushed by the winds off the Gulf. She ran up the stairs ahead of him and took the hidden key from behind the planter and started to unlock her door.

Tim stepped close to her and reached out to take her arm, pulling her to him and looking deep into her eyes. "I will miss you this evening," he said as his hand moved from her arm to the back of her head and his other hand gently reached under her chin, pulling her mouth to his. He kissed her slowly, brushing her rain-soaked hair from her face before his kiss grew stronger and more passionate. She kissed him back with a hunger she didn't know she had. She could not help it. Finally, this was the kiss of a man and it moved her.

"So, will I see you tomorrow?" he asked, tracing the side of her face with his finger.

"I hope so," she whispered. "I leave the day after."

He released her and simply said good night before entering his side of the duplex as she too entered hers.

Chapter Fifteen

Trust Your Heart

ONCE INSIDE ANNA STOOD, STUNNED, marveling at the kiss just delivered and wanting more. She walked back to the bedroom and picked up his sweatshirt she had not yet returned and once again held it to her face. It still smelled like him. She went into the bathroom to dry off. Anna ran her fingers through her wet hair and decided not to blow it dry but to let it dry naturally, knowing full well it would curl up. Looking at herself in the mirror, she slowly ran her hands across her chest, her T-shirt still wet and clinging to her stomach and her breasts, revealing her body through the almost transparent fabric, hoping he had noticed too. She took a towel and dried off before changing into jeans and a knit shirt. Comfort and warmth were what she wanted.

Anna went into the kitchen and turned on the teakettle before deciding to light a fire in the gas fireplace. The feel of autumn had crept in with the stormy evening. As the fireplace warmed the room and took the dampness from the air, she started to prepare her dinner. She boiled the shrimp she had purchased earlier that day and made a salad with the produce. Anna found that she missed Tim and the dinner they had shared the previous night. His warm and sincere spirit charmed her. It pleased her to know that there was a man who, unlike her husband, seemed truly interested in her and concerned for her.

As she ate her meal, she tried to plan for her future, deciding she could only take one step at a time. As soon as she returned to Atlanta, she would contact the attorney who came highly recommended by a friend. Anna thought of two nights before, telling John she was divorcing him, and the argument that followed.

"I am going to get away for a few days, John, I need time to myself to figure out my future," she announced.

"Your future?" John said mockingly. "What about my future?"

"It's seems you have already moved on to your future with your new girlfriend, and I am finished being made the fool. John, I am filing for divorce," Anna said calmly.

"I don't know that you are talking about," John said, trying to act perplexed. "If you leave me, Anna, I will make things very difficult for you."

"Come on, John, be a man and admit it. I found your emails to your lover. I found the condoms and Viagra you so cunningly hid in the bathroom. I know this is not the first time you have cheated on me, but I will tell you it's the last time. I am getting out while I still can," she continued.

"Anna, you are overreacting," he said.

"Really, John," Anna said as she walked to the family computer and read the email thread out loud. He and his paramour wrote of their plans to meet after work for "together time," of his unloving wife, and lamented the fact that a divorce would take months to reach completion, delaying the beginning of their new life together. They talked of the many "blessings" they gave each other and this would carry them through the time they would have to wait.

"Blessings," she said with sarcasm. "Such an interesting choice of words, an adulterous husband finds blessings with his mistress. Well here, John, you have my blessing, go to her, I am finished."

John stared at her, his mouth gaping open.

She hated that look. "Now I am packing a suitcase and leaving for a few days. I have talked with Will and Carrie already. They think I am going to Alabama to help a friend. I would like to keep it that way. I will be back late Saturday."

"No, Anna, you can't go, I have business," he said.

Anna interrupted, "I am not asking you, I am telling you, I will be home on Saturday. Whatever business you have, you will have to work out. And John, I will be filing for divorce as soon as I return."

"Where are you going?" he asked sheepishly.

"That's no longer your concern," she said, leaving the room to finish her packing.

Anna took the last bite of shrimp, got up from the table, and carried her dishes to the sink. As she loaded the dishwasher, she wondered just how stupid could he be, carrying on an affair with a woman from his office? Did he stop to consider the financial risk to his family if he got caught and fired? But, she reminded herself, he never thought of anyone other than himself; it just didn't matter anymore, she no longer cared.

"I've carried him as long as I can," she shouted out loud, to no one listening in the room. "I just can't do it anymore. I have covered for him, run interference for him, and fixed all the bad situations he has put us in, and never was there any consideration for me or for what I have done. He has no people skills, no empathy, and no warmth. I was always hurrying to fix and pick up behind him, to smooth over hurt feelings left in his wake. Covering for him, I lost myself. And now it's my turn to live my life!"

A large clap of thunder startled her. She walked to the bedroom, looking out the glass door to the Gulf, which was barely visible because of the heavy rain and darkening sky. She picked up a book from her bedside table, walked back to the warmth of the living room, and settled in under a blanket to try to read, but she could not concentrate. Shortly before ten, she heard a car door slam and her heart leaped. She heard his footsteps as he ran up the stairs and found herself hoping he would knock on her door. Instead, she heard his door open and close. She listened for a few minutes until no further sounds from him could be heard. Disappointed, she put down her book and decided to go to the kitchen to make a cup of tea. She chastised herself for acting like a schoolgirl, foolish for enjoying a crush that she did not deserve. Just whom was she kidding; he would not want her as flawed and unworthy as she was. She stopped herself in mid-thought: "No, this is the negative thinking I have to free myself from, the exact thing I promised myself I would not do anymore." She decided to knock on his door and trust her heart for the first time in years.

Chapter Sixteen

Tim's Lament

ANNA MADE HER TEA and turned off the lights in the kitchen, determined to go visit her attractive neighbor to see what the evening held for her. Checking herself in the mirror, she touched up her makeup and brushed her hair. She picked up her keys and the cup of tea and walked across the living room but before she reached the door, she heard a soft knock. She laughed out loud as her heart jumped. Tim was standing in her front door with a box in one hand and a bottle in the other. His face lit up when he saw her.

"Come in, out of this rain," Anna said laughing. "I was just getting ready to knock on your door."

"That pleases me greatly," he said, placing the box and bottle on her kitchen counter. "I am happy to hear we think alike."

Tim made himself at home in the kitchen, opening cabinets and looking for plates and forks.

"I brought some cheesecake from the restaurant. Hungry?" he asked as he moved on to looking for small glasses to pour them some port wine. He handed her a glass and carried the dessert to the coffee table in the living room.

They both sat on the sofa to eat the cheesecake as he discussed the dinner and visit he had with friends in town. The roads were terrible in the storm. While driving to dinner, he considered turning around and returning, he explained. But this dinner had been planned for weeks. He had not seen his good friends from Houston in a few years, and his desire for a visit with them compelled him to make his way through the thunderstorm and into Gulf Shores. He found himself rushing through the meal, anxious to return to her, and hoping she would be awake when he did.

"My friends are staying in Gulf Shores through the weekend, and have invited you back for dinner on Saturday, if you are interested," Tim said, as he cleared away their dishes. She smiled and reminded him that she was leaving Saturday morning to return to Atlanta.

"Perhaps I can persuade you to stay another day," he said as he sat back down next to her on the sofa.

"I don't think that is possible," she smiled. "I have just paid the rent until Saturday."

"You are welcome to stay with me," he said as his eyes twinkled with mischief.

"We will see what Saturday brings," she whispered.

"You would like them." He continued to talk of his friends Daniel and Susan Rutledge. "They were our closest friends, having moved to Houston shortly after we did. In fact, I met Daniel the first summer we were married, working on the oil and natural gas rigs out of Biloxi, and we later met up again after graduate school and continued working together for years in Houston until I decided to resume teaching after Barbara's death."

"When did you work offshore?" she asked him. Many of her friends had spent their summers working the rigs as well.

"It had to be the summer of 1979; I needed to earn more money to finish my master's degree. Working offshore provided the best money, but the work was exhausting. We spent two weeks on duty offshore and one week off duty. We still lived in Baton Rouge, but I would head down to Biloxi with a couple of co-workers for my shift. We arrived on Sunday afternoons and were ferried out to the rigs by boat returning on Saturday nights. I earned enough money in one summer to pay for my graduate work and Barbara's schooling as well. The stipend I earned as a graduate assistant during the year and Barbara's part-time jobs kept us eating with enough gas and rent money to make it to and from school. Other than that, we didn't seem to need much money. We had each other and that was enough.

"I was able to graduate on schedule and the job provided me with experience to continue in the petroleum industry after graduation. Barbara returned to art school to resume her studies after we lost the baby," he said slowly and with great hesitation.

"What? She lost the baby?" Anna interrupted. "What happened?"

"We never knew," Tim continued. "Just after we returned to Baton Rouge from our wedding trip here, she had a miscarriage. When I returned home from teaching that afternoon, she was bleeding heavily and waiting for a return call from the doctor. She had no way of getting in touch with me as there were no cell phones back then and I had our only car with me. I rushed her to the hospital but it was too late. She had lost the baby. Only a few days after our wedding trip to this beach."

"I am so sorry," Anna said softly.

"The hospital admitted Barbara overnight and I stayed by her side and held her while she cried, we both cried. There was no amount of comfort I could give her. All I could do was hold on to her and grieve with her. I promised her that I would never leave her side and in time, we would have a baby, another baby, all ours to love and raise together.

"But what about my family?" she asked over and over. She was so afraid that they would make her come home. I had to reassure her that we were married now; there was nothing they could do to separate us. When she recovered, together, we would return to her family and work things out.

"However, she was right to be concerned. When news of the miscarriage reached her parents, they demanded the marriage be annulled. In their view, she was young and had been led astray by an older man. This sin, in fact, was the cause of the miscarriage, as we learned on our Thanksgiving visit to Galliano a few weeks after Barbara recovered. They refused to listen to Barbara's pleas and her clear commitment to our marriage. The marriage was not legitimate. It had been performed by a Justice of the Peace and not in the Catholic Church, and must be dissolved. We offered to get married again, in the church. But this fell on deaf ears as well. And, it became clear to us then that no amount of persuading could change the minds of her parents. Barbara was warned that if she left the house that day with me, it would be the last day she would be welcomed home.

"I will never forget the look on her face," Tim's own face was soft with the recollection. "With a look of total peace and serenity, she took my hand and announced that she chose me. One day, she hoped her family would welcome her back home. But her new home was with me and she intended to live her life with me by her side.

"She kissed her mother good-bye and tried to do the same with her father, who refused her kiss. She stepped away shocked, but standing strong as she returned to me. 'It's time to go home then,' she said, as I wrapped my arm around her for strength and together we drove back to Baton Rouge.

"The strong woman dissolved as we pulled onto the highway. She buried her face in my shoulder and cried like a little girl. I had to pull off the road to console her. We spent Christmas break mending our souls and finding strength from each other. I encouraged her to re-enroll in school and find herself in her art again. She did so, and through her art, her spirit slowly healed. As a result, her art became inspired as all the emotions she carried flowed into her work and professors and local artist began to take notice of her. Her gift blossomed."

Anna wiped her eyes. "Was she ever able to reconnect with her family?"

"Yes, under regrettable circumstances," Tim answered. "About five years later, her father suffered a heart attack and stroke and died before she could reach his side. We were living in Houston at the time; I had taken a position at the corporate offices of a petroleum services company. The call came from her brother early in January and we rushed to the hospital in Thibodaux to join her family. However, by the time we reached the hospital he was gone. He had died a few hours before we arrived. Barbara was devastated, hoping he would forgive her for eloping. She had been the apple of his eye, a daddy's girl, his only daughter, but he had never forgiven her and had not spoken to her since that day.

"After the funeral services, we stayed a few extra days to help her mother pack up her father's belongings. I helped her brothers with some home repairs that were too difficult for a sixty-year-old woman to handle alone. Barbara and her mother revisited old photographs, home movies, and memories. Through laughter and through tears, they were again a family."

Tim stood up to refill his glass, motioning to Anna, but she declined, preferring to drink tea. "Barbara was pregnant again at the time and, of course, the nearing birth of a baby brought much anticipation and happiness back into her relationship with her mother and slowly the distance and hurt melted away," he said with a gentle smile.

"As we departed for our trip home, her mother hugged me and welcomed me to the family and even called me 'son.' When Hannah was born, Barbara's mother was there with us in the delivery room," Tim set his glass on the coffee table. "She became a lovely and devoted grandmother to Hannah and even charmed her way into my heart."

Tim released a sigh from deep within. "My daughter is so far away from me now, I seem to have no direction or ambitions any longer. I find that I have withdrawn from living and seem more often to be going through the motions of just simply getting through my day, rather than actually participating in my life.

"Does that make sense?" he asked rhetorically. "I no longer feel alive, or have a desire to do anything other than work and go home and hide myself away, watching mindless television shows and waiting for time to go to bed, so I can wake up and relive the same scenario over again. I have been so lost in my loneliness, I find myself pouring over photo albums of my family, when we were together, when we had each other, my daughter and wife smiling back at me through old photographs, some now yellowed with age. I sit for hours with tears streaming down my face, just longing to have those days back, longing to see my wife once again and hold her close to me." Tim lifted his glass to his lips to hide the sadness he had just revealed. But it was impossible. He walked into the kitchen to retrieve the bottle, this time bringing it with him on his return to the sofa. He reached to pour Anna some more, but she waved him away. "Have you ever wished to have one day back, Anna, just one day?" he asked her in a serious tone. "What would that day be for you?"

She knew immediately: the night of the Jubilee, thirty some odd years ago. She told him how she and the boy she had loved so much had started to make love, how they had been interrupted that night, and how she and the events of the evening prevented him from resuming. For years, she had dreamed about that night and in the dream the outcome was different. She fervently wished she had been able to finish what they had started, to allow him to make love to her, as he had so wanted to do, as she had so wanted too. Emptiness and longing revisited her dreams of the encounter that never was to be. Over the years, she tried to remember the feel of him holding her, the warmth of his skin on hers, his loving touch, his taste, his smell.

"I have wished over and over again, countless times to relive that one evening," she whispered.

She often wondered how her life would have been different. Would she have gone away to college? Would the rape have occurred? Would they have married? Would she have let him slip through her hands forever? So many questions were left unanswered and still plaguing her. Instead, she had the life choices she had made afterward: putting too much distance between herself and the young man, moving away to college, and the fateful deed she still blamed herself for. What hurt the most was the fact that she believed she had betrayed him. She was never to know the honesty and pure love she would have given to him, and he to her, if he had been her first partner. "I let true love slip through my hands, forever, and the outcome of that one night may possibly have changed my life. Who is to say that whatever might have come from it would have been a fleeting moment of pleasure or a lifetime of joy, I will never know," Anna's voice quivered with tears.

Tim wiped his face with his hands. Sounds of heavy rain and thunder outside had brought a dark and serious tone to the room. "I would relive the night Barbara died, because she died without me," Tim said with utmost chill to his voice. His face was ashen, his voice faltering, his wrist shook as it held his glass.

Stunned by his revelation, Anna sat up, grabbing his hand.

"I can't, I can't go there," he said so faintly, but he turned his head, searching Anna's eyes, his wounded soul called to hers and found peace and acceptance in her eyes.

"Only if you want to, Tim, you can," Anna ran her hand through his hair.

His pain and sorrow was so deep, so raw. She caressed his neck, not saying a word, but for this small moment as their worlds collided, honesty emerged and forced each one to look deep into their souls for answers and to face what they had avoided and found too difficult to otherwise reveal.

"Anna, I was there, but I failed her, she died alone," Tim said as he threw back the contents of his glass.

"What do you mean?" Anna asked, encouraging him to go on.

He breathed in a deep, slow breath, trying to regain his composure but also trying to decide if he could visit this, the deepest regret of his life, and share it with her, a new friend.

"My wife lived for several days after the horrible car accident. I was by her side. As I prayed for her life, she never knew it. Barbara was in a coma for three days and did not know I was there." He reached over and poured another glass from his bottle. "Barbara had just left a showing in Baton Rouge. She called me, thrilled with the many glowing reviews from fellow artists she admired greatly and numerous orders she had received for commission pieces. I was in Houston with Hannah; Barbara was heading on to Natchez, Mississippi, for a weekend art fair and exhibition there before heading home. She left just before dusk. Rain was in the forecast but was not expected to move in for a few hours. She should have been in her Natchez hotel room before the weather became an issue. The front moved in more quickly than forecasters anticipated, and Highway 61 was a two-lane road, winding and hilly, not the interstate as she told me earlier.

"I can only speculate about what happened as the weather turned and the night skies darkened. The police report said a deer ran out in front of Barbara's car, which she hit, causing her to lose control and spin off the road and crash into a tree just north of St. Francisville. The carcass of a deer was found near the accident site.

"A nurse at the Baton Rouge hospital recounted once driving that highway and being terrified by the dozens of pairs of eyes glowing back at her from the reflection of her headlights. Almost as if the trees had eyes, she explained.

"A passing car came upon the wreckage several minutes after the accident occurred. There were no witnesses. Police and state troopers arrived on the scene and a life flight helicopter was called in to fly Barbara back to Baton Rouge. The closest hospital equipped to handle trauma."

Tim took a sip from his glass and wiped his eyes on his shirt. "I arrived from Houston as quickly as I could, flying to Baton Rouge on the first morning flight. When I saw Barbara, she looked so peaceful, childlike, and calm. Equipment and machines surrounded her, with tubes invading her body, her arms, her nose, and her chest. Monitors beeped everywhere, shattering the very peace that emanated from her. She looked like an angel. She was so serene; it was almost like she wasn't even there at all and just the shell of a woman remained. All I wanted to do was to hold her, protect her, and save her from the serenity that terrified me to the core of my being because deep within me I knew she was already gone. I wanted her free from all that invaded her, to see her alive and vibrant as she had always been. Happy to see me there in the room, jumping out of her damnable hospital bed, and throwing her arms around me as she did whenever we had been apart. But she didn't even know I was there."

He continued with great difficulty, struggling to hide his tears. "I stayed by her bedside for three days. Anxiously awaiting the many visits from the doctors, hopeful that perhaps on the next visit the prognosis would be better. But, the doctors never delivered such news. I read to her, talked to her, recounted the many lovely memories of our life together, the joys of parenthood as we watched our baby grow, the secret love we shared in college before our wedding, and of course, I talked of her beach. I promised to bring her here in November, once she recovered, as was our anniversary tradition."

He was barely audible now, through his heavy tears. "Late in the evening on the third night at the hospital, I was overcome with exhaustion. I had not allowed myself to sleep, fearing that I would miss her when she awoke from the coma, fearing she would squeeze my hand and I would miss it. But, on that fateful night, I fell asleep by her side, holding her hands in mine, as I slumped over the chair, my head on her hospital bed. The signals and loud beeps from the many monitors woke me as the nurses came running into the room. She was gone, Anna, she left me while I slept. She slipped away from me and I didn't know it. Did she try to say good-bye by smiling at me or patting my hand? Did she murmur something to me as she departed my life forever? I have never forgiven myself for not being awake during that final moment. She didn't hear now much I loved her as she left this world and my life."

Anna sat silent as Tim walked to the back door, opening it to let the cool air rush in. For a moment, she thought he was leaving, but he turned back to her. "The doctors assured me that she would not have done anything other than to drift off to death as she peacefully slept. But I have always wondered."

Anna rose and hugged him, not knowing what to say or do. She closed the door to stop the chill and searched the room for a box of tissues. Now she was crying too.

"Two days after Barbara's death, I returned home to my daughter and all the sadness of the memorial service and our lives without her mother. Barbara had always been clear about cremation, it was her wish, and so I returned home with her ashes and longstanding instructions of what she wanted done with them."

Anna stared at him, wide-eyed, half expecting the words that came next.

"Her beach," he stated simply. "Her beach."

"Anna, I could never bring myself to do it, never," he said with a sigh. "For the last four years, I have returned here each November, but I could not release her, I just couldn't let her go. I know full well this is what she wanted, what we always said we would do, I just never thought I would be faced one day with actually having to do it. I figured I would go first, or by some twist of fate we would go together, leaving the task to our daughter."

"Do you have them with you now?" Anna whispered.

Tim nodded.

"Tim, does your daughter know this beach?" she asked.

"Yes, of course she does. She was part of the many visits here when she was growing up," he answered, looking baffled by her question.

"Then wait. There is no time limit on how and when you let go. Talk to your daughter, let her know about Barbara's instructions and your desire to be released here as well. Have Hannah promise you that when the time comes, she will return for both you and your wife. Together you loved this beach and ocean, together you return to it and become a part of this place forever."

He considered her suggestion for a moment before shaking his head in his hands. "This is my burden and something I must do alone. I believe my wife would have wanted me and me alone to grant her final wish. And, until I do, I honestly don't know that I can start living my life again, or forgive myself for the guilt I carry to this day."

The room fell silent and Tim carried his glass to the kitchen sink. "It's one-thirty," he said to Anna. "It is time I head back to my side and to bed and let you get some sleep."

He leaned over the sofa and kissed her softly on the cheek before slipping out into the night. She locked the back door as she heard the door to his half of the duplex close.

That night she prayed that one day she would find someone she could give herself to, someone who would love her, as she had known all those years ago; a relationship that allowed her the security and safety to love and to trust. Tonight, she finally realized that the means to set herself free resided only in her heart. Until she dealt with the devastation left behind by that vile act thirty years ago, she would never have an honest and intimate relationship. She must learn how to trust again, but this time it was her own self that she needed to trust. But with trust she had to first find forgiveness. This was the first step, forgiveness, a simple word to say and yet at times impossible to do. But she knew deep in her soul it was time she learned how to forgive herself for the rape and the series of wrong choices she had made as a result.

Chapter Seventeen

The Children

IT WAS MID-MORNING WHEN ANNA AWOKE and she smiled, seeing the time on the clock. For the first time in years, she had slept in. The discussions into the wee morning hours and the sound of the beating surf and rainstorm helped her lose all concept of time as she slept through the night. She wondered how Tim felt this morning and hoped he was not suffering the effects of too much alcohol. Fueled by the port wine, he had poured his soul out to her, feelings he had not easily shared. Anna was thankful she had only taken a few sips of the wine, preferring to drink tea as she listened. Goodness would come from his releasing his long pent-up feelings about the death of his wife and his belief that he had failed her.

She stepped out of bed and pushed open the sliding glass door, welcoming in the bright sunlight that replaced last night's rainstorm. Her head was clear this morning and she felt rested and ready to relish the remaining hours here, this last day on her beach. The brilliant light bounced off the sand and water, beckoning her to come down to the water and walk. She turned on the coffee pot and made a small breakfast, carrying both out to the bistro table on her deck. The other side of the duplex was dark and quiet. She wondered if he was still sleeping. She looked out over the water, the waves still rough from the strong winds of last night. Her eyes caught a little boat in the distance. "Sail freely, sail on," she thought, as she finished her coffee. "Sail on to new waters, and all those discoveries still waiting for you." As she watched, the November winds fueled the blue boat with pretty white sails bouncing across the croppy sea. She whispered, "Sail on brave ship, sail on. I am like you, battling the waves and wind, the setbacks and the storms. May I emerge as gracefully as you, navigating the unseen pathway of my life."

Anna carried the dishes inside and set them in the kitchen sink. She got dressed hurriedly, determined to walk the beach without being heard, seen, or detained. The company of her new friend had been a delightful gift but she needed time to herself. Instead of turning east toward the bay and fort, her morning way took her west toward the high-rise condos, the planned communities, and concrete swimming pools reaching across the remaining sand dunes closer and closer to the shoreline and the water's edge.

The previous night's storm had washed green and brown seaweed to the shore, over and around which Anna carefully stepped. The sand had been beaten flat by last night's heavy rain. Circular impressions embedded in the sand by the raindrops were crushed beneath her feet as she walked. Broken shells, driftwood, pebbles, and the carcass of an occasional dead fish mingled and clung to the seaweed littering her path. Disarray and confusion washed ashore in tangled sea foam seemed to be a metaphor for her life. Eventually, the debris would find its way back into the Gulf, pulled and sucked back into the water by the rising tide. The water and the sand were the only constants here, the surf beating a constant rhythm on the receiving shore. Cleansed and renewed by nature, this beach, as the beating of the waves, never ceased.

She looked at her life, a tangled mess. The only constant that remained for her was the only one that truly mattered— her two children. Whatever disappointment or challenge life sent to her, nothing could rock the foundation of the love she had for the little boy who once climbed into her lap with golden cherub ringlets and pudgy round fingers pointing, "Look, race-car, Mommy. Airplane, Mommy." How he had adored his mother, running to her for loving when hurt, together laughing through pages of books, running down the hall in footed pajamas to climb into bed with her each morning to snuggle.

His elastic-waist blue jeans and T-shirts with trucks and trains, red sneakers and baby clothes, she saved in a box under her bed, unable to let go of when they became too small. Special toys and his blanket were treasures she stored away as well; these she saved to return to him one day, perhaps when he became a father.

As she walked, she remembered the hours she had pitched baseballs to him and leaping with joy as he rounded for home off the grand slam he just delivered. Their days spent in the park pretending to be pirates or dinosaurs, picnics and adventures to the bay house. How had he grown so quickly? Where had the years gone? When he was a baby, friends and family would always say, "Enjoy these days, they go so fast." However, as true as the statement was, during the growing years, she missed the fact that time was indeed racing by.

Through childhood illnesses, she had rocked him day and night if it meant just giving him some comfort or relief. The monsters under the bed or in the basement she chased away. He always turned to her to give him the confidence and reassurance he needed to allay whatever problem he was wrestling with. A tender and gentle child, he loved his mother and preferred her to his father to soothe the challenges of his life.

How quickly the words of family and friends became true; he was suddenly a young man passing his driving test and living the trials of teenage life, trying to be cool and fit in. High school years were upon him and college loomed ever closer. He stood four inches taller than her and when she hugged him, she realized she was hugging a young man, he was no longer a child.

She remembered how difficult it had been to drop Will off for kindergarten. She had tried to be brave, though her heart was breaking as she turned to leave him with new friends and his teacher sitting cross-legged in a circle saying their names by turns. In the car, her tears flowed as she set down her camera filled with images capturing this milestone. She thought of him in preschool and the trauma that ensued after a bee chased him on the playground. Filled with fear, every night he prayed for rain so his class would not have to play outside and he would not have to encounter that mean bee again. She calmed his fear too, and before long, he was running and chasing friends across the playground, forgetting the bee altogether. Big steps in her life and his, and now she faced the challenge of telling him that she was leaving his father.

She worried more about the reaction from her daughter to the pending divorce. Anna believed her son would understand. Will was older and his relationship with his father had taken a mature turn. John had traveled extensively while Will was young. As a result, father-son activities such as camping trips or adventures were rare. Anna filled both roles during Will's youth. What relationship existed now between father and son was on an intellectual level and more as a peer than a parent. Will was indeed a man and found himself comfortable relating to his father in this way.

Her daughter, Carrie, four years younger than her son, was the apple of her father's eye, and she would struggle with the news more, Anna suspected. She was a confident child, open and loving, tenderhearted and observant. She loved her brother dearly and looked up to him for encouragement. Her father doted on her, pampered her, and Carrie understood how to work this to her advantage.

Yearning for a daughter came soon after her son started school. Suddenly Anna started noticing babies everywhere, but knew she could not have another child due to the complications from her son's birth and subsequent hysterectomy. She loved and adored her son and was happy in the gift of him, but something tugged at her heart.

Will announced he wanted a brother or sister at around age five. He talked of nothing more, even sharing the wish with Santa Claus as the thing he wanted most for Christmas. Because of his loving spirit, he needed a sibling, the gift of a brother or a sister, the joy of growing up together. He was not meant to be an only child. This was the best gift she or Santa could ever give him.

Soon she started to notice little girls on park swings, pigtails flying, holding on tightly as their mothers pushed them from behind. Anna wanted one more chance at motherhood. She adored her son; she wanted a daughter to love as well. In her heart she felt God was showing her that another child awaited her. Her eyes and heart were open, as the calling grew louder. She recalled a lengthy discussion in a sporting goods store with an older mother carrying a bi-racial baby girl. The child was all dolled up in the pinkest of outfits with a pink satin bow clipped in her curly black wisps of hair. Her children, the woman explained, were grown and out of the home, and so she chose to foster a child. Soon she realized she loved the baby too much to imagine sending her on to another home, so she had proceeded with the adoption. Now this lovely girl of about eight months in age was all hers.

A local newspaper advertised an upcoming adoption seminar for international adoption. Orphaned children around the world were in desperate need of homes. With the sound support of her husband, her family was completed in a land far away. A daughter, soft and tiny for a one-year-old, was placed in her arms. Her son was no longer an only child.

What joy this new baby brought to their home and to her life! Anna marveled at the ease with which this beautiful baby fit into their lives, truly as natural as if Anna had given birth to her. There was no difference; in her eyes, she was meant to be the mother to both children, growing up together as brother and sister, knowing they were truly loved. Anna watched as Carrie blossomed. She sang, she danced, and she loved playing dress-up in glittering princess outfits designed by her mom. Twirling in full skirts to watch the ruffling around her knees when she stopped. A charming and beautiful girl, full of loving hugs, settled into her family with ease.

A smile crossed Anna's face as she recalled times the children would bicker or fight. Far from irritating, she found it amusing. The children had each other and the true experience of growing up together. They each had a sibling and no one could take that away from them. When she was dead and gone, they would have each other to rely on or turn to as a touchstone to their past and one day, the promise of grown-up visits, extended family, cousins, and family reunions.

Sometimes, especially around Carrie's birthday, Anna wondered about the birth mother who for whatever reason had to give this baby up. Pain gripped her heart, understanding that the biological mother would never know this enchanting child. Never hear her giggle or sing, never braid her hair or help her with homework, hold her through tears and kiss her hurts away. This gift was hers, one she truly treasured and would be ever thankful for.

Anna knew it was inevitable that the children would be scarred in some way by the fact that their parents were parting ways and moving on, but she prayed that they would not blame themselves, assume responsibility for the breakup, or feel any less loved by either parent. She would move heaven and earth to be certain that they knew they were loved, and she hoped John could show this to the children as well. The divorce was waiting for her tomorrow. Tomorrow she would head home to encounter an unknown she never expected to face.

As Anna walked farther west, she lamented the numerous high-rise condominiums swallowing up the coast. Her beach was in jeopardy of falling prey to the continuing growth. She was thankful for the fact that Alabama state parks would forever hold a parcel of her beach in its protection and prevent it from being further developed. Although change would inevitably come to her beach, just as the coming life change was now a reality for her, she could always return here and find some remaining evidence of her youth.

She turned around and headed back toward her duplex as the sun warmed the day, which she suspected was long passed noon. Anna removed the T-shirt she wore over her bathing suit and slowly strolled at the edge of the surf. Should she and John discuss the divorce with the children together as a family? Or should she have a private talk with each child first as a foundation for a family discussion? As the water lapped around her ankles, she felt perhaps the latter would be the best way. After a few days home, she would begin to discuss the upcoming divorce with her son first, closely followed by one with her daughter. Next, she and John must sit down together and speak with them in a way that was nonthreatening and to be honestly clear that the break-up was not their fault and they were deeply loved by both their mother and father. While their parents would no longer live together, the children's needs would always come first and they would always know that they were loved.

Anna continued to wrestle with her thoughts as she made her way back. She was not yet at peace with this issue or how to settle these concerns that worried her deeply.

In front of the duplex were a large turquoise beach umbrella and two folding chairs. Tim was sitting in one chair and the other was empty. He waved her over. He had a small cooler at his feet and a canned soft drink in his hand. She joined him under the umbrella and sat down in the empty chair.

"Good morning, Anna, or afternoon as it must be by now," Tim said, with a hesitant and searching look in his eyes. He did not seem looking for her forgiveness, but more for affirmation, a sign that she had understood and accepted the raw feelings he had trusted to her in his deepest moment of sadness and honesty. "I did not feel much like running today, a bit of a headache this morning," he said, trying to mask his concern with a smile. "I had hoped my behavior last night didn't make you want to pack up and head back to Atlanta a day early."

"Oh no, not at all. My heart went out to you and I was honored that you trusted me enough to share such deep emotions from your life. I could never judge anyone for being honest," she said. "I certainly would not want to be judged or thought ill of for being vulnerable." She could see that he was relieved by her answers.

"Perhaps I had a bit too much to drink and the alcohol fueled my thoughts and loosened my tongue. Anyway, you now know the story of my adult life and my deepest regrets, my loneliness and inability to move out of the past. I guess, like you I need to move on with my life, having been so paralyzed after losing my wife." He continued, "I especially need to make a new life for myself now that Hannah has married and moved away; I am a widower with an empty home. This could be why I was meant to meet you this week, to help me realize that I too must start living again."

He opened the cooler and asked her if she wanted a soft drink. She smiled and took the drink, pleased to have it after her long morning walk.

"What time is it, by the way?" Anna asked. "I have lost all track of time today."

"I came out to sit here at about one o'clock, or probably thirty to forty-five minutes ago, so my guess is that it is close to two," Tim answered, rubbing his wrist as if there was an imaginary watch there. "Anna, let's ride into Gulf Shores for a late lunch or early dinner, depending on what time we get there. Do you remember the Pink Pony Pub? It is still in Gulf Shores by the public beach, and they always had the best fried crab claws in town."

She laughed, remembering the pink building, and the crab claws, "I can't believe it is still here and has not been swallowed up by condos or a hotel chain. Yes, let's go. That sounds like a great way to send me back to Atlanta, revisiting an Alabama landmark. But I will only go if you promise to order some coconut shrimp as well as crab claws. As I remember, they were the best I have ever eaten."

"Can I persuade you to stay until Sunday, if we get two orders of the shrimp?" he said, smiling a wicked smile at her before taking another drink from his soda can.

As they talked and watched the surf from their folding chairs nestled in the dunes, Anna found herself laughing openly and often. She felt completely free and at ease around him. She had found more of herself in just a few days by revisiting her past and enjoying the new friendship she had with Tim. She had not expected to regain her self-confidence so quickly, but the protective wall she had placed around herself had begun to erode away. Perhaps just knowing they would both be leaving this beach soon and going their individual ways gave her the ability to be totally upfront and honest with him. There was no time for game playing or pretending to be something other than her true self. She had nothing to lose. He was here, she was here, and they owed each other nothing.

"I set Barbara free this morning," he said, breaking a silence and stopping her thoughts.

Anna turned to him in surprise, but there was nothing she could say.

He raised his hand and pointed out over the Gulf to a sailboat on the horizon. He smiled at her and took her hand in his, as though he had been reading her mind and understood her thoughts and feelings, as she too understood and honored his. She watched the sailboat, the same boat she had noticed earlier in the morning, on its return voyage home to a waiting harbor. Silently, they enjoyed the sun, sand, and each other as the afternoon drifted away.

Chapter Eighteen

The Clearness of Night

THEY ARRIVED AT THE Pink Pony Pub in the late afternoon, and the restaurant was alive with activity and customers. They were seated at a table for two at the front windows giving the greatest view of the Gulf. Beachcombers strolled along the shoreline as the evening began to take hold and the round orange glow of the sun sank lower and lower across the western horizon before disappearing into the sea.

They placed their order for crab claws and coconut shrimp and the waitress filled their glasses. Tim lifted his beer mug and toasted her. He laughed out loud to be drinking the same evening after suffering a dull headache in the morning. But this was their last night. He was feeling festive and the headache had long since passed. She raised her wine glass to meet his mug and they smiled at each other as he said,

"To a lovely week." They talked and laughed and watched the darkening Gulf waters as they waited for their food to arrive. When their meals were placed on the table, they both agreed to sample and share the crab claws and shrimp. To her delight, the food was wonderful, and tasted just as she had remembered.

A band started playing shortly after seven and the music was loud, making it difficult for them to hear each other. Tim got up and paid the bill and together they walked outside on the deck facing the water and down the wooden ramp to the beach below. After Anna stopped to remove her shoes, they walked to the shoreline. Other couples strolled up and down the beach and families with children played in the sand as they walked past. There was much activity on the Gulf Shores beach for a Friday evening in November, more than on their private beach some twenty minutes away. Both commented on the activity, condos, restaurants, and development, before deciding to turn around and return to their more private beach. Tim threw his arm around Anna's shoulders as they made their way back to the pub and his car waiting in the parking lot. They drove through Gulf Shores, back to Fort Morgan Road, and their duplex waiting on the eastern end of the peninsula.

"I will meet you out on the deck in a few minutes," Tim said as he pulled into the carport.

Anna set her handbag down on her kitchen counter and removed her sweater. The evening air was milder than the last two nights had been. There was little wind off the Gulf tonight, adding to the warmth of the evening. Perhaps the rainstorm of last night had brought in a warm front, Anna speculated. She hadn't paid any attention to the weather, the news, or television for days and realized she was completely out of touch with the outside world. Stepping out of time and reality for a few days had given her the respite she so needed. She was taking a bottle of water out of the refrigerator when she heard tapping on the back of the house. She walked to her bedroom and opened the sliding glass door to discover that the latticework dividing the two sides of the deck was removed and pushed off to one side of the duplex. Tim was grinning from ear to ear.

"I found a way to open the divider. I felt certain there had to be a release to swing this open and sure enough, here it is," he said, pointing to a spring-loaded latch hidden behind the potted plants. "I was sure there would be a way to open up this area, enlarging the deck, as I imagine this home is rented out a lot for families, large groups, and reunions."

He went back inside and came out to the deck with his iPod speakers set in a dock station. "What would you like to listen to?" he asked.

"Just pick out whatever you would like. But make sure it is not as loud as the band at the Pink Pony."

"Okay then, let's visit the sounds of the 1970s," he said as he selected the playlist, "since that is the era when we both found this beach. We can relive our youth through the songs of our generation."

She took a seat on his cushioned patio chaise and watched as he cleared the furniture from the center of her side of the deck and placed it up against the walls of the duplex.

"What are you doing?" she asked with amusement, watching him as he worked.

"Why, I am clearing a dance floor, of course." He smiled the wicked smile she had come to know over the course of the last few days. "Would you care to dance?"

She didn't have time to answer; he had already taken her hands and was pulling her to him in an embrace while the music softly played in the background, dulled by the rhythm of the surf below. He held her so closely now, playing with her fingers as he held them in his hand, his other hand holding her waist, pulling her closer to him. His lips swept across her forehead and down through her hair to her ears. He whispered slowly in her ear, "Have you decided to stay one more day or must you still leave tomorrow?" With the heat of his words tickling and warming her ears and neck. "Can I convince you to stay with me until Sunday?"

As she enjoyed the warmth of his breathe on her ear, she said, "No, Tim, I have to leave tomorrow, I have to see my children, I promised them."

"Of course, I understand, and although I am disappointed, let's make the most of this last evening together," he said, lifting her chin and searching deep into her eyes.

She noticed the warmth in his chocolate brown eyes rimmed with lines of character, but still a boyish look from the slant of his brow downward, almost like a puppy. Warm and loving, sincere and beckoning, his eyes revealing his fondness for her. She found him deeply attractive, ageless. A longing inside her grew as he continued to look deeply into her eyes.

He released her chin and ran his hand to the nape of her neck and reached his lips down to hers, kissing her slowly as he continued to sway to the background music. She responded to the warmth of his lips and mouth by wrapping her arms around him, her fingers answering in soft reply, dancing across his back. Song after song, they danced before he broke his hold on her and reached to the table for his water. Anna picked up her bottle of water and walked to the deck railing and looked out over the water.

"It is so beautiful here. I never grow weary of this place. Once again, the evening is enchanting,'" he said. "And you make it even more so, Anna."

From his iPod playlist came the song that reminded her most of the boy she had loved and memories came pouring back with the opening piano notes, as Boz Scaggs gently sang, "We're All Alone."

"This song holds more special memories for me than any other one song from the time I spent with my first love. This was 'our' song and being here and hearing it now, transports me to another time years ago when he was mine. Tim, over and over again we would play this on the eight-track player in his car." She smiled and laughed, "To this day, I cannot hear this song without recalling the hours we spent dancing or making out to this song and the album *Silk Degrees*; it was the soundtrack from our time together, my youth."

She looked out over the beach as the melody and lyrics swirled around her, stirring feelings of love for a boy she had never forgotten. "What was once, I lost, but still to this day, I carry him in my heart," she said softly, as if to herself.

"The night is young, and the surf is calling us, listen. Do you hear it, Anna?" he asked.

She shook her head, yes, wanting to visit her beach one last time before leaving in the morning. "Let's walk together," she answered him, setting her water on the table.

"Then we will return here after, to dance under the stars." He took her hand and led her through his side of the duplex. Together, they descended the stairs and headed out for the water, running like two young children as the cooling sand was kicked up by their bare feet.

The warm Gulf water lapped at their ankles as they walked silently for a while in the direction of the fort.

"How could he let you go, your husband?" Tim asked, not allowing her time to answer. "What kind of man fails to see the beauty of you and the love you never got to give away, what kind of man? How did he not see it? You need to be encouraged to be free to love, to give without fear of rejection. I see so much in you that you have hidden away to protect yourself. I am glad you are leaving him, Anna, you will be amazed at what your life will bring to you. Promise me that you will allow yourself to be truly loved again, as you described to me in your youth. You will find it out there, I just know, because you deserve so much more than what you found in your marriage. I see a beautiful woman standing here with me, starved for love, denying herself all these years, denying her needs. Don't do it any longer, Anna. Life holds so much more happiness for you."

She had never admitted it to herself, but Tim said it so perfectly. She was indeed starved for love. So many times through the years she had ached so for love, for validation, to be held and surrounded in the security of a deeply intimate relationship. For too many years now this feeling had eluded her. Still, the longing continued to haunt her, visiting the deepest of sleep through dreams and memories of a fleeting time in her life when she had known without question that she was loved. Tonight, she knew in her heart that Tim was right. She had to go out and find it.

He wrapped his arms around her tightly and said, "I hope this does not offend you, but damn it, Anna, I cannot understand how someone could not see the love in you. He will be shocked when you leave and he realizes the magnitude of what he once had, never nurtured, and lost forever. You are truly a gift of a woman and I just can't understand him not seeing that, not at all. But I have said enough about the sadness of your marriage, I will not bring it up again."

"You give me encouragement to face the unknown and to do what I have to do," she assured him. "I have ignored my needs in my life for far too long, and tomorrow a new chapter begins. But for tonight, let's just walk here together and listen to the music of this beach."

"A place we both love," he said softly.

The night was clear and the stars danced and flickered across the sky. He raised his hand to point out a shooting star off in the distance. Red and white lights glittered and flashed off the oil and gas platforms on the horizon and sparkled across the water. The crescent moon cast a silver shimmer across the waters of the Gulf. They neared the point and as always, she searched for the western shore but it was not visible, instead being swallowed up into the darkness of the evening. The lights on a passing cargo ship were all she could see on the bay. But she knew he was over there somewhere, as always a distance away, unaware of her nearness to him. Unaware that she still cared. They stood still, looking out over the dark water. It was time to turn back.

"Stay with me tonight, Anna," he whispered into her ear, although there was no one around to hear the urgency in his request. "I am not ready to let you go, please stay with me tonight." He turned to face her and she saw the warmth and longing in his eyes.

"Yes, Tim, I will stay with you," Anna replied. "Yes." Tim, she thought, you have no idea how I long to stay with a man. Yes, she was thrilled that this man wanted her, this caring, sensitive man. More importantly, she finally had a chance to prove to herself that she was desirable and wanted by someone. Tonight for this man, she was still beautiful and desirable, just as she once had been more than thirty years ago.

Anna stopped in front of the duplex and looked out over the Gulf, as if to say good-bye. "I am always so sad to leave here," she said. "I feel like I am leaving a piece of my heart here each time I have to leave. So many wonderful memories live here for me. Now, I have you to add to that list. The joy of meeting you, and sharing our love of this beach, I will never forget."

They smiled at each other with complete understanding of the magic they shared on this private beach.

Chapter Nineteen

Desire, Nothing Else Considered

LEAVING THE SLIDING GLASS DOOR OPEN, they found their way to the bedroom on her side of the duplex. He slowly began to undress her, stroking her warm skin with his hands and his lips as more of her body was revealed to him. His touch lingered, slowly exploring her, unhurried and skilled. He understood a woman's body and the need she had for him. His lips found her neck and moved slowly to her breasts. A feeling she had so loved and long forgotten, but this evening she cleared her mind of everything other than the feeling of his body, his touch, and the pleasure he seemed so determined to give her. He returned to her mouth with deep kisses, searching and probing. These she returned with an honesty she had long suppressed. There were no words spoken, just the deepest of sighs as he knew what she wanted and just how to please her. This he made clear through his slow and deliberate reactions to her as wave after wave of pleasure enveloped her body. Tonight was about her and his desire to satisfy her completely.

The surf provided the background music of their lovemaking long after the playlist on his iPod played out. The soft breeze refreshed the air in the room, blowing through the open door. There was no one else around to invade their privacy.

He lay next to her, stroking her hair when they had finished. Whispering to her how beautiful she was and thanking her for the gift she had just given him. "Anna," he whispered, "you are the only one I have been with since my wife, I will never forget this evening or you. Please stay with me until Sunday, when I leave here too, I fear this will be a lonely, miserable place if you leave me. Must you go tomorrow?"

"I have to," Anna answered softly.

"Yes, I do know that, and I understand. I will miss you so," he said, as he buried his face in the nape of her neck, moving his free hand across her body, continuing to savor her and every bit of time he had left with her.

Tim was first to fall asleep. She continued listening to the sounds of the surf and his breathing. For once in her life, she had allowed herself the pleasure of a man, without guilt, without regret, finally admitting to herself that she deserved this and vowing never again to deny her own needs. It was time to seek out the love she had missed all these years. As she fell asleep, a smile came to her as she considered the possibilities of the new life that awaited her.

She woke a time or two during the night, feeling the warmth of the man lying beside her. He stirred too. Feeling her awake, he pulled her to him closely, not wanting to let go of her, and then together they drifted back to sleep.

The bedside clock read 6:52 as she peeked from the pillows, aware that she had to pack and get ready for a day of travel.

Tim sensed her movement and groaned. "No," he said and reached to turn the clock so she could not read the face of it. The morning air was cool and damp so he pulled her to him for warmth and once again began to stroke her body with longing and desire. She felt a stirring within her and his arousal became evident as well. One last time, he took her to a place of great pleasure, slowly savoring each other until they could give no more. For another hour, they lay there together in her bed, trying to gather the strength to begin the day that ultimately meant her departure, not wanting their magic to end, but knowing that it must.

"I have to get up and get ready to go," Anna said.

He placed one finger over her lips, and kissed her with such gentleness before saying, "Yes, it is time."

He reached for his pants. After he dressed, he stopped to pull the siding glass door closed, taking note of the clear blue morning sky.

"I will start your shower for you and then make us some coffee," he said.

"Coffee would be great, but only if you join me after," she said with a laugh in her voice.

"By all means. The coffee will be started in a flash," he laughed.

She was already in the shower when he opened the door to join her. Lather from the soap and shampoo floated down and tickled their skin as they clung to each other, not wanting to face the inevitable.

"You know that eventually the warm water will all run out," Tim joked. "And the rental company will find us here, frozen together, when they come here tomorrow to clean."

Anna laughed, "Yes, I suppose you are right, one of us needs to step out then." With one final kiss, Tim left the shower, grabbing a towel before setting out for the kitchen to make her a cup of coffee.

He carried the cup to her and said, "I will let you dress and pack as I run next door for my clothes. I will make you a breakfast in my kitchen and be back to help you load the car."

When he finished preparing breakfast, Tim carried it out to the bistro table on the deck and knocked on her door to let her know it was ready. He went back inside to retrieve the coffee pot when she opened her door to the deck.

The morning was clear and the blue sky mirrored the waters of the Gulf. She had always loved this time of year, as the last of the warm weather waned over south Alabama before winter took hold.

"I have more coffee," Tim said as he stepped out onto the deck.

Together they enjoyed the breakfast and the dazzling beauty of the sun on the blue Gulf waters, which sparkled like diamonds.

"I love this beach so, and it is difficult to have to go and leave this all behind," Anna said with a sigh. She reached across the table and took Tim's hand, thanking him for breakfast. He pulled her up, wrapped his arm around her shoulder, and walked with her to the railing of the deck. Together they looked out over the water.

"Yes, it is a wondrous place, made more magical by you," he whispered in her ear before lifting her chin up and kissing her softly. "I am sorry you have to leave today, so very sorry."

After a long moment, Anna moved to clear the dishes away.

"No, I will handle this once you have gone," he said. "Go on ahead and finish what you need to do to get on the road and I will help you with your suitcases."

Anna went back into her bedroom and was gone for a few minutes before returning to the deck.

"I suppose I should return this to you," she said, holding Tim's gray sweatshirt and laughing. "Otherwise, you might remember me as a thief."

"No, no, keep it, it actually looks much better on you," his eyes flashed with amusement.

Anna looked down at the sweatshirt knowing this was a memory she wanted to keep. "Thank you, Tim," she said, before returning inside and putting it in her suitcase.

Tim followed her inside.

Tim slid two tote bags onto his shoulder and carried her heaviest suitcase down the stairs to the carport. As he unlocked the tailgate of her car, she walked back through the duplex one last time, scanning for overlooked belongings and silently saying good-bye. She took one last look from the bedroom, over the Gulf and the beach below before closing and locking the sliding glass door. She walked through the living room, gathered her sunglasses, and stepped outside, pulling the back door closed behind her. She locked the door and dropped the house keys into her jacket pocket. Tim placed the last suitcase in the back of the car and closed the hatch, giving it an extra push, making sure it was closed securely, although it was obviously tightly shut.

"You are good to go." He was obviously trying to hide the fact that he was saddened by her leaving. "I have never been good at saying good-byes," he whispered in her ear as he pulled her close one last time. "I will never forget these few days we shared. I came here to remember and heal, never expecting to find such a dear friend. I never once dreamed such joy would find me again. Thank you for sharing this moment in time with me."

Anna noticed tears in his eyes. When one escaped down his cheek, she reached out to wipe it away as he had done for her just a few days earlier. He, too, had touched her heart deeply in a time of great uncertainty.

"You have my phone number, my email address, and my heart," Tim continued. "Promise me, if you need anything, even just to talk, you will call me."

"I promise," she told him as she hugged him closely.

"If you decide to venture this way next year, I will be here as I always am during the first week in November," Tim said. He lifted her chin and looked into her eyes and said, "Don't lose sight of how beautiful you are, inside and out. You deserve to be happy. You deserve to be loved. Be strong as you go and find it."

"I will, Tim," she replied. "I will."

Together they walked around to the driver's side of Anna's car. She opened the door, tossed her purse inside, and set the keys on the driver's seat. She turned to him one last time and he pulled her into a strong embrace. Gently, he kissed her good-bye. Anna touched his face softly before climbing into the car.

As she pulled out of the driveway, he climbed the stairs to his side of the duplex and waved her off, blowing one last kiss.

Chapter Twenty

Letting Go

SHE REACHED THE MAIN ROAD back to Gulf Shores, but turned the car left up the western road and into the grounds of the state park that led to the fort. The parking lot was busy with cars lining up to take the mid-morning ferry across to Dauphin Island. From her car, she could see the ferry approaching its loading dock on the return trip from the island.

Anna parked her car in the parking lot and walked down to the beach fronting the fort, one last time. She picked up a broken oyster shell and threw it, watching as it skimmed across the calm water. The sky was so bright and blue; she almost could not make out the land on the western shore for the glare off of the water. But it was there, always beckoning her. She could see the outline of Fort Gaines on the distant tip of Dauphin Island and the landmass stretching northward toward the city of Mobile.

She found herself staring out over the water to the other side, searching for him as she always had. Wondering where he was, searching for him but never finding him, just as so many fantasies and dreams of him had played on her mind throughout the years. She could not recall a time in her life when he left her memory or her dreams. He had stayed quietly in the background, continually haunting her for all these thirty years. As a result, she had never completely given away her heart or her soul again; they remained with him. But now the time had come to let go. If she was to move on with her life, she realized that she must give up the unfulfilled dream of him.

"Good-bye," she whispered to him somewhere on the western shore. "I must leave you where you belong as a lovely memory of my youth. I have loved you all these years, but you haven't known it and don't need to learn now. Because I once loved you truly, I know I can love again. It is time that I set myself free to find what the rest of my life holds for me. You were my first love, my youth, and my past, now I must find my future. And so today, my dear, I release you from my heart and forever say good-bye."

A seagull shrieked overhead, a mullet jumped from the water, a blue heron stood tall along the shoreline as sandpipers scampered by. She removed her sunglasses and wiped the tears from her eyes. It was time to go home.